# THE PURPLE ROSE

Christi R. Walsh

ISBN: 1502371413
ISBN 13: 9781502371416
Library of Congress Control Number: 2014916970
CreateSpace Independent Publishing Platform
North Charleston, South Carolina

*"Artists who seek perfection in everything are those who cannot attain it in anything."*
—*Gustave Flaubert*

# 1

She was the one. He couldn't believe he had finally found her after all this time. He watched her as she left the bookstore. She was perfect. Her long dark hair with touches of auburn ran down her back and ended at her waist. He guessed her to be about five foot four. She was slim and looked like she was in good shape. Perfect.

He continued to watch her as she walked down the main street of Portland, Oregon. Portland had almost three million people living in the metropolitan area. It gave him plenty of room to roam when he didn't want to be noticed. He could blend in no matter where he went. His whole life, nobody had ever really seen him, and that included his whore of a mother. Soon, though, *this woman* would notice him.

He got out of his car and started to follow the woman. He followed her until she turned into a local coffee shop. He wondered if he should go in. He wasn't worried about her noticing him. He waited five minutes to give her time to order and sit down, and then he walked in. It wasn't a large space. With just a few people in it, it was crowded. No one noticed him coming in, and that included the woman.

She sat at the corner table, drinking something hot. Her hands were wrapped around the cup as if she were cold. He wasn't sure why she would be cold. It was a hot afternoon for the season. Weather around Oregon was unpredictable, though it was usually raining. But today was warm and sunny.

He walked up to the counter and ordered a regular black coffee. He didn't go for all those fancy drinks available now. He turned and sat at a table near her but not too close. He didn't want her to notice him. Not yet. Soon enough she would know him. For now, though, he was content to just sit and watch her.

She was quite extraordinary. Her skin was baby smooth. He imagined it to feel like velvet. He couldn't wait to find out. He was starting to get excited just thinking about it. He needed to calm down. He didn't want to spook her. Her eyes were dark blue, like the deepest part of the ocean. She had high cheekbones and full lips that were made for him to kiss. She wore hardly any makeup, but she really didn't need to. His mother used to cake on the makeup, and he had always thought she'd looked like a clown. She had told him men liked it, though. So naturally, he had hated it.

The woman had a book open and was reading. He assumed it was the book she had just bought at the bookstore. He needed to find out what it was. He liked to be prepared. As if sensing somebody was watching her, she lifted her head and looked around. He quickly lowered his head to avoid eye contact. He watched her out of the corner of his eye. After deciding there was nobody watching her, she lowered her head and continued to read.

It was time for him to go. He got up, left the coffee shop, and headed across the street. He hid behind a lamppost. He waited for another thirty minutes before she came out. She turned right and started walking down the street. He stepped away from the post and started following her on the opposite side of the street. She stopped suddenly and looked around. She looked in every direction, and he wondered if she sensed he was there. He stepped into the doorframe of a retail shop. He watched her through the shop's glass window. After a few moments she shrugged and continued on. He gave her a head start and then moved out from his hiding spot to follow her. He had to know where she was going. He couldn't lose this one.

She stopped at a bistro. He thought she was going to go in, but instead she went in a door next to the restaurant. He could see apartments were above it. He knew this must be where she lived. He debated whether to go in. Not knowing how many apartments were up there, he was afraid he might run into her in the hallway. If he waited and didn't go look, though, he wouldn't know which was hers. He decided it was worth the risk. If he ran into her, he could just say he was looking for a friend's apartment.

He stepped out into the street, crossed it, and came to the door. He was happy to see he didn't need a key. He opened the door and went in. The stairs led directly to the apartments. Once his eyes adjusted to the dimness of the building, he could see multiple apartments above. He headed up. The hallway was about twenty feet long with two apartments on both sides. Unlike his place, the building was well maintained and clean. He lived on the east side of town. People didn't like to go there, but he liked it. He could do a lot of things in his neighborhood, and people either didn't notice or didn't give a damn. All the apartments here had numbers on them. He was just getting ready to head down the hallway when a door at the end of the hallway on the right opened.

There she was. She came out of the door and into the hallway. He turned and shot back down the stairway. He heard a knock on a door. A door opened, and he heard talking. He slowly went back up the stairs, just high enough to see over the steps. She was standing at a door and talking to somebody. He couldn't see the person, but he sounded like a male. He sounded young. It sounded as if they were flirting with each other. Warmth spread across his face, and sweat broke out on his forehead and neck. He listened more and realized that the male was doing all the flirting. *Stupid punk,* he thought. Didn't he know she was way out of his league? He listened to their conversation.

"Hey, Nick. I think I got a piece of your mail."

"No problem, sweetheart. I'll have to thank the mail carrier for that later."

She laughed, but he could tell she wasn't buying into Nick's charm.

"So, what do you say to us going out and grabbing some dinner?"

"I don't think—"

"Come on, Kate. You have to eat, right? It's not a date. Just two friends having a meal together."

Her name was Kate. He liked it.

"You're right. I have to eat, and it would be nice to have some company."

"That's my girl. Let me just grab my shoes, and I'll come knock on your door. See you in a few?"

"That's fine." She turned to go back to her apartment.

*What the hell? She's going to go out with this guy?* He didn't get a look at the man, but his voice told him he was a player and not worthy of her. He turned and headed back down the stairs. He left the building and crossed the street. He would wait for them there.

Ten minutes later they came out of the building and turned left. Again he followed on the other side of the street. The man looked about twenty-five. He had brown, overly long hair like a hippie's. He was slim, and it looked as if he spent some time in the gym. Most women would probably find him attractive, but his Kate seemed immune. She was a smart girl. They picked a restaurant not too far from the coffee shop. It looked to be a Thai restaurant. They entered the building and were immediately seated. He stayed across the street to watch them.

It looked as if Nick was doing all the talking. Didn't he know that was not how to impress somebody like Kate? He continued to watch. An hour later they got up and left the restaurant. They turned back toward her apartment. They seemed relaxed and were walking slowly. They came to their apartment building door and entered. Again he gave them a few minutes before he approached the building. Very quietly, he entered and listened. He could hear them upstairs.

"I had a nice time. Thank you, Nick."

"Sweetheart, it was my pleasure. You need to get out more."

She laughed. "I have work, school, and a lot of homework. I don't have time to go out."

"You know what they say about all work and no play?"

"I know, but I have only one semester left. I just want to finish and move on to the next stage of my life. It's been a long haul, and I'm ready for the next adventure. Thanks for tonight, though. I'll see you around."

It sounded as if she were leaving to go to her apartment.

"Why don't you come in for a drink?" he heard the male say.

That made him snicker. The boy still thought he had a shot with her. *Stupid boy.*

"Thanks, but I don't think so. I'll see around, I'm sure."

"Sure thing, Kate. And remember, if you need anything, I'm just down the hall."

He heard both doors close. He left the building and started back to his car. It was dark now. He looked around to make sure no one saw him leaving the building. When he reached his car, he unlocked it and got in. Sitting there, he thought about Kate. He wondered what his plan of action should be. She was special and deserved much, much more than the other women. A smile crossed his face. He knew what he was going to do. It was perfect. *Kate, I'll be coming for you. Soon you'll be mine.*

Kate sat in her apartment and tried to get motivated to write her paper on the different social aspects of the "now" generation. Normally, she loved forming thoughts and trying to put them down on paper, but right now the act held no appeal. She looked around at her apartment with pride. It wasn't large. The kitchen and living area were all one big room. There was a bedroom, bathroom, and laundry area down the hall. She had worked hard to get where she was now. She was going to school, and she had a good job at the bookstore. She loved to read, so it was perfect.

Her life growing up, however, had not been perfect. She had survived, though, and had come out on top. She had lived through foster home after foster home. Most foster parents had been good people but some not so much. When she'd turned eighteen, she'd left and never looked back. That was seven years ago.

It took her several years to save enough money to start school. She had worked several jobs and stayed in studio apartments to save on rent. Nick was right. She didn't go out a lot, but she never wanted to spend the money. Like she had told him, she also just didn't have the time.

When she finished school, though, she intended on changing that. With her degree in social services, she could find a good-paying job. She had picked social services because she had been in the system for so long, and she thought she could make a difference. The kids who ended up in the system weren't usually bad kids—just kids people had forgotten about. She wanted to make sure every child had a fair shot. She knew she couldn't save them all, but she was willing to try.

When she focused on her paper again, she went back to look at what she had already written. She felt out of sorts today. When she'd left the bookstore, she had felt the hair on her neck stand up. Then she'd felt it again after she'd left the coffee shop. It had felt as if eyes had been on her. She knew it was crazy, but she couldn't shake the feeling. She had intended to stay in tonight and write her paper, but when she had looked through her mail, she realized she had something addressed to Nick.

She liked Nick okay, but he really wasn't her type. He was attractive enough and even sweet, but he just didn't do it for her. At first she didn't want to go, but then she remembered the feeling of being watched. And dinner had been fun; it had taken her mind off the earlier feeling. However, now she had to get this paper done. She was never late turning in her papers, and she wasn't going to start now.

Two hours later she finished her paper. She rose from the couch, stretched her muscles, and headed for her bedroom. A noise made her stop and listen. She could have sworn she had heard something at her front door. She was standing there debating what to do when she heard it again. *Standing here frozen like a statue isn't going to take care of the problem,* she thought.

She turned and headed for the front door. Maybe it was Nick. When she reached the door, she looked through the peephole. She wasn't scared, but she wasn't stupid, either. She didn't see anyone out there. She wondered if she should open the door. If she didn't know for sure what the noise was, she knew she would never go to sleep, and she had an early class tomorrow.

After fifteen seconds of arguing with herself, she finally opened the door. At first glance she didn't see anybody or anything. However, when she looked down, she saw a purple rose in front of her door. She bent to pick it up. It was beautiful. It was large for a rose, but the color made it amazing. She had never seen a purple rose before. It was gorgeous. She brought it to her nose and smelled it. It had a sweet fresh-flower smell. She frowned when she saw a red spot resting on one of the petals. Then gasped when she realized what it was.

It was blood. She dropped the flower and froze. *What should I do? Call the police? And tell them what? I received a rose with blood on it? Am I overreacting? Maybe Nick brought it. Why would he give me a rose with blood on it, though? It doesn't make sense.*

She knew she was going to have to go over to his apartment and ask. If it was him, she would let him know she didn't appreciate it. Did he think it was funny?

When she had worked up her nerve, she picked up the flower carefully and headed to Nick's door. She knocked and waited for him to answer. By the time he did, she was in a temper.

"Hey, sweetheart, what's going on? Twice in one day you're knocking at my door." He stood there smiling at her.

Kate held the rose up just inches from Nick's face. "Did you leave this at my door?"

Nick reached for the flower. "A rose? It's nice, but it wasn't me. I'll take the credit, though, if nobody else does." He laughed. Then he saw her expression. "What's got you so upset? Most women like getting flowers."

"They don't if they have blood on them."

Nick looked at the flower again. "It looks like a rose, Kate."

"Look at it, Nick. Look closely," she demanded.

He looked at the rose and shrugged. "I see a red spot. How do you know that's blood?" he asked. "Is this what's got you so worked up? It just looks to me as if you have an admirer."

*Maybe Nick's right*, she thought. She had just assumed it was blood. It could be anything.

Kate looked at Nick. He looked sincere. *Great*, she thought. *I just made a fool of myself.* "Sorry, Nick. It just freaked me out a little bit." She turned pink. "It's probably nothing. You're right. Maybe it isn't blood." She didn't know how to seem less like a fool. She looked up and smiled sheepishly at him. "I'm sorry to bother you. It must be my overactive imagination. When I was walking home from the bookstore earlier, I was reading and I felt…"

Kate stopped talking. All the blood drained from her face. Nick grabbed her. "Hey, Kate, you look as if you're going to pass out. Come inside. Let me get you some water."

Kate stumbled into Nick's apartment. It was the same layout as hers but messier. Clothes were everywhere. He helped her to his couch and pushed aside a couple of pieces of clothing. He gently pushed her down to sit. She stared ahead blankly.

Nick brought her a glass of water and sat down next to her. When she didn't reach for it right away, Nick took the glass and put it her hand. "Kate, you're scaring me. What's going on?"

Kate didn't respond. *It has to be a coincidence.* The book had just come in, and it looked interesting. Kate had told Mags, the bookstore owner, she'd wanted to borrow it. Mags was the sweetest lady on the planet and always trusted Kate to "borrow" books and bring them back.

"Okay, Kate. You have to tell me what's going on or I can't help you," Nick said.

She turned to Nick with frightened eyes. "I brought home this book from the bookstore today."

Nick looked at her with confusion. "Okay, what does the book have to do with the flower, though?" Nick asked.

"The name of the book is *The Purple Rose.*"

"Okay," Nick said again, drawing the word out. "I don't think it means anything, but obviously you do."

Kate blinked. "You don't think it's a little weird that I bring a book home today called *The Purple Rose,* and then a few hours later there's a purple rose on my doorstep?"

She wondered if she should tell him about the feeling of being watched today. Would he think she was even crazier? *Maybe I am overreacting. Take a breath, Kate. Nick is right. It could mean nothing.* Somehow, though, she didn't think so. "Do you think I should call the police?"

Nick picked up her hand and held it between his. "It's obviously upset you. If it would make you feel better, then call the police. I'm not sure what they can do, though."

Kate thought it over. Nick was right. What could the police do? She had no idea who would have left the rose, and maybe it had nothing to do with the book. Something felt off, though. Kate pushed herself to her feet. She shook her head and looked down at Nick. "I'm sorry I barged in on you. I'm better now. The rose just spooked me."

Nick stood and took her hands. "If it would make you feel better, you could stay here tonight."

Startled, Kate looked at him. He was giving her a suggestive look. She realized he was trying to be funny. She smiled. "Thanks, Nick, but I think I would be safer in my apartment."

"Sweetheart, you're killing me. Seriously, though, if it would make you feel better, you could stay here."

Kate turned and headed for the door. "No, I'm fine now. I didn't mean to get angry with you."

"It's okay. You can get angry with me anytime."

Kate laughed and reached for the doorknob. "Nick, my friend, you are an endless flirt."

Nick grinned. "I try."

On an impulse Kate reached for Nick and gave him a hug. She was not normally a hugger. Kids who grew up in the system weren't generally used to hugs. Nick hesitantly gave her a hug back. *Obviously, he isn't used to hugs either,* Kate thought. "Come on. I'll walk you to your apartment," he said.

Together they made the walk back. Nick said good-bye, and Kate went inside. But when she was in her apartment again, she realized she had left the rose with Nick. She thought it was just as well. She didn't want it anyway.

She was feeling restless now. If there was ever a good night to start drinking, she thought it would be tonight. Instead she made tea. She still felt a little spooked. She checked the locks on her front door and checked all her windows. In her bedroom she checked the window that opened to the alley below. She looked down. She didn't see anyone lurking or anything else creepy.

"Get a grip, Kate," she said aloud. "You're freaking yourself out."

Turning back from the window, she went through her nightly routine and crawled into bed.

In the alley below, he watched Kate through the window. He knew she couldn't see him. He was in the shadows behind a large trash can. He wondered how she had liked his surprise. He was sure she had loved it, and he smiled. He wondered if she had made the connection with the book. It was a stroke of genius to come up with the rose in so little time. He had had to go back to the bookstore to find out what book she had purchased. As it turned out, she worked there. The old woman in the bookstore hadn't wanted to cooperate at first. However, he had told the woman that Kate was his friend, and Kate had told him he should go in and ask the manager about the book she had borrowed. Kate said she would know the book he was talking about.

He wasn't worried about the woman being able to describe him. He had changed his appearance so nobody would recognize him. He could change his appearance so his own mother wouldn't recognize him. He snickered at that thought. He could go in tomorrow and talk to the woman, and she would never know he was the same person she had talked to yesterday. The badge always helped too.

He had found a purple rose, which had not been easy in such a short time. He was a clever and determined man, though. He always got what he wanted, and he wanted Kate.

# 2

The next day Kate was still a little spooked. She got up and went to her early class. Sleep had not come easily the night before. She had tossed and turned for hours, so she was running on only a couple hours of sleep.

Somehow she made it through her class. She was even able to follow what the professor was saying. She left class and headed for the bus stop. She had to wait only a few minutes for the bus. She had never had a car. It was too expensive, and she had no place to park it anyway. Living downtown made everything except school convenient. The bus worked fine for school, though. Once she was back in her neighborhood, she headed for the coffee shop. She'd been too late this morning to stop. She would need a triple if she wanted to make it through the rest of the day.

She stepped up to the counter and greeted the barista. She was an attractive petite girl around twenty. She was friendly and always knew Kate's drink.

"Hey, Sarah."

"Hey, Kate. How's it going?"

Kate yawned. "I'm good, but I think I need a triple today."

Sarah smiled. "Coming right up."

Kate stepped aside so the customer behind her could order. As she waited for her drink, Kate started to get that feeling again. She felt as if somebody were watching her. Trying to act as casual as possible, Kate looked around. She didn't see anybody looking at her or even remotely interested in her. *This is ridiculous. It's just your imagination, Kate. Suck it up.*

When her drink was ready, she grabbed it and headed for the door. She stopped with her hand on the doorknob. Outside she noticed a guy standing across the street. That was no big deal, but it seemed as if he were looking at her. It was hard to tell. He was wearing sunglasses, and she couldn't see his eyes.

Kate looked around the coffee shop. She wondered what she should do. What could she do? Either call for help or not. What if she was wrong, though?

*Come on, Kate. Put your big girl pants on.* She looked back toward the street. The guy was gone. Kate let out a breath. *See, Kate. Just your imagination.* With one last look at the spot where she had seen the man, she turned the knob and pushed the door open.

Kate headed home to work on a paper that was due next week. She could get a head start on it before she had to go to work that afternoon. She opened the door to her building and headed upstairs. She was thinking about the paper she had to write. She wasn't paying attention to where she was walking, and she stepped on something in front of her door. Kate looked down. She was standing on another purple rose. Crying out, she jumped back. She stared at the rose. It was the same kind of creepy purple rose as the one from yesterday. Too afraid to touch it, she left it there.

She turned and started for Nick's apartment, but she realized he was probably not home. He worked at a bar across town at night, but during the day he worked in a retail shop down the street. Kate tried his door anyway but without success.

Again she wondered what she should do. *There are laws about this, right? Stalking?* She decided she would go to the police station instead of calling 911. She didn't think this would be considered an emergency. Feeling good about her decision, she grabbed her phone out of her bag and looked up where the closest police station was. It was within walking distance.

When she entered the station, she started to rethink her decision. Handcuffed people were being escorted through a set of doors down the hall. Behind a glass wall, men and women were sitting at desks. Kate noticed that the employees at the station were mostly men. They were either on the phone or typing on computers. Kate had never been in a police station before and hadn't known what to expect.

Not sure what she should do, Kate stepped up to the counter in front of the glass wall. She waited for the officer behind the desk to raise his head. After a few moments he looked up at her. He was in his fifties with a bald head and a belly that needed to see the gym. His kind eyes kept her from turning around and walking out the door. "How can I help you, miss?" he asked in a deep voice.

Now that it was time to speak, Kate choked on the words. "Um."

The officer was looking at her and waiting for her to continue.

"I think I'm being stalked," she blurted out.

Kate looked at the officer, waiting for him to either laugh or tell her there was nothing they could do for her. Instead he started looking around. "Just one moment. I'll find a detective for you. What's your name?" he asked.

"It's Kate Riley," she said, still surprised.

"Have a seat over there." He was pointing to a row of chairs lined up against the wall.

*Well, so far so good,* she thought, and took a seat. *They haven't laughed me out of the building yet.*

Kate was now fidgeting in her chair. She had waited for half an hour, and still nobody had come to talk to her. The longer she waited, the more she regretted her decision to come. *They are going to think I'm crazy. Maybe I am.* She stood. But just as she was reaching for the door handle to leave, somebody called her name. "Kate Riley?"

Now she was committed. She turned. "I'm Kate."

A man was walking toward her and extending his hand. He waited for Kate to shake it. "I'm Detective Rowe."

He was an attractive man in his early thirties with a full head of dark hair. He also had kind eyes. Kate figured she had picked the station that required its officers to have kind eyes. *Kate, you're losing it.* She smiled at the detective.

She knew most men found her attractive. It was probably the long hair. People had told her she had a heart-shaped face, but she always thought her chin was too pointy. She saw interest in the detective's eyes but didn't respond to it. Maybe someday somebody would make her want to.

"Why don't you come to my desk," the detective said, "and we'll see what we can do for you."

Kate followed the detective through the gate that separated the lobby from the area behind the front counter. He stopped at a desk in the back of the room and pulled a chair out for her. After she was seated, he sat in his own chair. "Now, what is it I can do for you?"

Kate hesitated. She might make a fool out of herself. She was spooked enough to take that risk, though. "I think I'm being stalked."

The detective leaned back in his chair. "Why do you think that?" he asked evenly.

Kate had no idea what he might be thinking, but she went through her story. She talked about how she had felt as if she were being watched, about the book she'd borrowed called *The Purple Rose*, and about the two purple roses showing up on her doorstep. Kate swallowed. "There was blood on the petal of the first one."

"Are you sure it was blood?" he asked.

"I don't know for sure, but it looked like it."

"Can I see it?" he asked in the same tone as before.

"I left it at my neighbor's last night," she said hesitantly. "I thought maybe he had left it, but it wasn't him. I must have forgotten it there."

"So, you don't have the rose?" the detective asked.

"No." Kate shook her head. "I'm sorry. I'm not making sense." Kate took a deep breath. "I came back from class today, and there was another one outside my door."

"Okay. Can I see *that* one?" the detective asked after a moment of hesitation.

"Sure. It's at my place. I didn't want to touch it in case there were fingerprints or something."

Kate saw the amusement on the detective's face. *Great. He thinks I'm silly.* She was surprised then, when he stood and grabbed his keys. "Show me the way."

She followed him to his car. He opened the passenger door and waited for her to get in. It was a short drive back to her apartment. The detective didn't say anything, so Kate decided she shouldn't either. Once they'd arrived, she took him upstairs and walked down the hallway to her door. She stopped. She looked at the detective with panic in her eyes. He frowned in confusion. "What's wrong?"

"The rose is gone. It's not here," she said, and looked frantically around. "I left it on the floor. I didn't touch it." Kate didn't know what to think, but then something occurred to her. "Wait. Maybe Nick picked it up." She started walking toward Nick's door.

"Who's Nick?" the detective asked.

"My neighbor." Kate stepped in front of Nick's door and knocked. No answer. She knocked again, but there was still no answer.

"Is this the same neighbor with whom you left the rose from last night?" she heard the detective ask. The detective was looking at her strangely.

*Oh no. He thinks I'm making this up.* "I'm not lying." She was practically yelling. "There was a rose last night and again today outside my door."

"Kate, I believe you, but without the roses there's not a whole lot I can do."

She thought he sounded sincere. "When Nick comes home, he can tell you there was a rose. He saw it and touched it." She sounded desperate. *Damn. Why didn't I pick up the stupid thing and bring it with me? Because,* she answered herself, *I freaked out and didn't want to touch it.*

"Okay. When Nick gets home, bring the rose to the station. Then I can have it tested to see if the substance on it is blood. Maybe there's something we can learn from it. Until I have something in hand, though, we're going to have to wait."

Kate knew he was right. "Thank you, Detective, for at least coming back with me. I know how this looks, but I promise I'm not crazy or trying to get attention or anything like that."

He smiled at her. "I don't think you're crazy, Kate. Unfortunately, though, like I said, we'll have to wait." He reached in his back pocket and pulled out his wallet. He handed her a card. "Here. If you need anything or if something else happens, give me a call." Kate took the card. "Come to the station when you have the rose." He smiled at her one last time and left.

Kate stood in the hallway for another few moments before going back to her apartment. She opened the door, went in, and looked around. She didn't see anything out of place. She turned the bolt on her door and headed for the kitchen. She thought drinking was looking better and better. She sighed and made tea. Looking at the clock, she noticed she had only an hour before she had to be at the bookstore. *So much for starting my paper,* she thought. She wouldn't be able to concentrate right now anyway.

Instead she plopped down on the couch and thought about her situation. The rose was gone, but anybody could have picked it up. If it wasn't Nick, maybe it was one of her other neighbors. The people across the hall were married. They seemed friendly enough, but she had never really engaged in a conversation with them. She didn't think they would have picked it up for her and given it to her later. The unfriendly woman across from Nick was in her seventies. Kate knew she wouldn't have picked up the rose. It had to be with Nick. Could Nick have come home after his day job and seen it lying there? Maybe he had put it in his apartment so she wouldn't freak out again. She didn't blame him if that were the case. She figured that had to be it. Feeling better, Kate started to get ready for work.

Across the street he waited for her. He wondered if she liked the second rose. He waited to see what she would do. She came down shortly after going upstairs. He noticed she wasn't carrying the rose. Where was the rose? Where was she going? He followed her. She had walked only a couple of blocks when she stopped in front of a building. It was the police station. Why would she go to the police station? He didn't know, but he was going to find out. He waited for her to enter. He went in not long after her. He saw her sitting in a chair and looking around. He was too clever for her to notice him, but he couldn't just stand there staring at her. He saw a door marked STORAGE. He headed for the door and hoped it wasn't locked. He tried the doorknob and smiled when it turned in his hand. He entered and left the door open enough to see her. She was so lovely, but she seemed nervous. After a while a man went over to her. He said something to her, and she stood and followed him to a desk at the back of the station. That was not a problem. He flashed his badge to the officer at the front desk. The officer barely looked at it before he waved him through. He walked to an empty desk that was close enough for him to hear. He couldn't get too close. Was she saying something about being stalked? She couldn't be talking about him. How could she think he was stalking her? He loved her. His anger rose to the surface. He would just have to show her how much he loved her. Then she would understand. She would understand she was his. Kate and the detective talked about going back for the rose. He smiled. He knew what to do.

Kate was a few minutes late to work that afternoon. She was never late, and it bothered her that she was. She tried to apologize to Mags, but Mags just smiled and patted Kate's hand. "Oh, dear. Don't you worry about it. You're never late, so you must have had a good reason today."

Mags didn't ask for that reason. Kate didn't even have a reason except that she was anxious and nervous. Kate tried to go about her work as if everything were fine. A couple of hours later, Mags walked up to her. "Oh, I almost forgot to ask you. Who was that gentleman you sent to see me about *The Purple Rose?*"

Kate looked at her. Her heart was pounding. "What gentleman?"

"You know, the one you sent here yesterday. He was a nice man but maybe a little pushy," she said disapprovingly.

Kate tried to hide how upset she was. She didn't want to worry Mags. "What did he look like?" Her voice shook, but Mags didn't seem to notice.

"You don't know whom I'm talking about?" She was frowning.

Kate shrugged. "I've told a couple people about the book." She hoped that sounded plausible.

"Oh, he was medium height, blond, and kinda pudgy in the middle. Is that ringing any bells?"

Kate wanted to scream. *No!* "Must be one of my school friends," she said instead.

Mags seemed to accept this answer, and moved on. *Now what, Kate? Go back to the police? Call Detective Rowe? No. Not until I get the rose from*

*Nick.* He hadn't come home by the time she'd had to leave for work. She would have to get it later.

Kate tried to get involved in her work, but her mind kept wandering. Who was this guy? What did he want? She was more determined now to get the rose from Nick and see the detective.

She eventually got through the rest of the day. At closing time Mags came over to her. "Dear, I have a dinner date with my friend at six. Do you think you can close up tonight?"

"Sure, Mags. A male friend?" Kate asked in a teasing voice.

A pink hue surfaced on Mags's cheeks. "Oh, he's just a friend, dear," she said, flustered.

"Well, then of course I can close up."

Mags swatted her arm and smiled. "Quit teasing."

After Mags left, things were quiet. Kate looked around the bookstore. One customer was left in the store. Once that person left, Kate could close up, get home, and see if Nick was there. While doing her paperwork, she glanced up when the last customer finally left. She was moving toward the door to lock up when the lights went out. Kate froze. *What's going on? Maybe it's a power outage.* She saw lights on across the street. *It could just be this side of the street,* she reasoned with herself.

On shaky legs she started for the door again. She heard a noise behind her. Kate whipped around but didn't see anybody. It was too dark. She frantically looked around and tried to see anything. She saw a shadow move, and she stood frozen with fear. A shape started to form in the darkness. "Hello, Kate." It was a whisper. Kate still couldn't move. "Aren't you going to say hello?"

"Who are you?" Kate asked, terrified. He was close. She wondered if she could make it to the door. It was better than just standing there. She started backing up.

"Don't be afraid. I'm not going to hurt you."

"Then come out of the dark and talk to me like a normal person." He moved again but didn't completely come out of the shadows. She couldn't see a face.

"I'm not ready to do that yet, Kate. I just wanted to know if you liked my surprises."

She didn't know what to do. She still needed to get to the door. Once she was out, she could run anywhere except there. If she could keep him talking, she figured she might make it. "I really don't like surprises," she said, and moved for the door.

"Kate, I'm asking you nicely to stop," he said in a deadly voice.

Kate did as she was asked. "What do you want?"

"I told you, Kate. I want to know if you liked my surprises."

"I already told you I don't like surprises," Kate said much more boldly.

"Well, we're going to have to change that. I have a lot more surprises for you."

Not waiting any longer, Kate swung around and rushed for the door. But before she could reach it, the man grabbed the back of her hair and pulled. Kate cried out in pain. He pushed her against the wall. Pinning her tightly there, he whispered in her ear. "Kate, what am I going do with you? I just wanted to say hello. You don't want to make me angry. Do you?" He pulled her hair again.

She was trapped. She couldn't move. He had her pressed up against the wall so hard, she could hardly breathe. Then she noticed something. She could feel his erection pressed against her back. Bile rose in Kate's throat. "Relax, Kate. I told you I wasn't going to hurt you," he said as if reading her mind. "But you are a beautiful woman. A man can't help but enjoy what's in front of him."

Kate tried to move again. He laughed mockingly. "Do you think that's helping, Kate?" Kate went absolutely still. "There. See? It's not so bad. I just want you to notice me."

Kate tried to keep her voice calm. "Okay. So, why don't you come into the store tomorrow? Then we can talk." *Like hell,* she thought.

"Because you haven't noticed me yet. But soon, Kate. Very soon you will."

Before she knew what was happening, he threw her to the floor and walked out the door. Kate was trembling so hard, she didn't think her legs would hold her. She sat in the dark for a few minutes until she was able to stand. She walked to the door to lock it, but her hands were shaking so badly, it took a couple of tries before she heard the lock engage. After she'd locked the door, she went to the back room to get her phone from her bag. She dialed 911, told the dispatcher what had happened, sat back down on the floor, and waited for the police.

# 3

The rest of the night was a blur. The police came and took Kate's statement. She told them about the purple rose and about the feeling of being watched. They listened but made very few comments. She had asked to speak to Detective Rowe but was told he wasn't available. The police called Mags to let her know what had happened at the store. Kate didn't want them to, but then she figured, Mags had a right to know.

After everything, Kate just wanted to go home. As if reading her mind, a young uniformed officer came up to her. "Ma'am, I'll take you home now."

She looked up at him but didn't really see him. She stood, and he put his hand on her back. *He probably thinks I'm going to pass out or something.* He was heading for a police car parked at a curb near the bookstore. She stopped him and told him she was just up the street. So they walked to her building. He opened the door and took her up to her apartment.

Kate stopped in front of Nick's door. "Do you mind? I want to see if my neighbor is home?"

"Not at all."

Kate knocked on Nick's door. She waited for a few moments before giving up. She didn't think he would answer, but she had to try. "I guess he's still not home." Kate started for her own door. She stopped in front of it.

She was still wondering where Nick could be when she realized, embarrassed, that the officer was waiting for her to get her key out.

"Sorry," she mumbled, and she searched through her purse. She got the key and opened the door.

"Would you mind checking to make sure everything is okay in there?" She hated the way her voice had shaken, but she couldn't help it.

"Sure, ma'am. You wait here." The officer smiled and went in. After a few minutes he came out and said everything looked fine. "I checked all your windows, and everything is secure." She thanked him and went to shut the door when he put his hand on it to stop her. "If you need anything or something doesn't seem right, don't hesitate to call us."

Kate nodded and closed the door. She turned from it and just stood there looking around. She tried to convince herself there was nothing to be afraid of. The officer had said everything was okay. She didn't think she would ever feel safe again, though. She slumped to floor and started crying. The sobs shook her shoulders. She knew this probably wasn't helping, but she couldn't stop.

*Why me? Did I do something to make this guy think I wanted his atten-tion?* Kate thought back over the last couple of weeks. She couldn't remember saying anything to anyone that would be even close to flirt-ing. That wasn't her. Maybe he was a customer. She couldn't think of anyone, though.

She dried the last of her tears, got up, and prepared for bed. Tomorrow she was going to see Detective Rowe and demand he do something. She didn't care if she had the roses or not. The police needed to do something.

For most of her life she'd been alone, but tonight she felt truly alone. She didn't have any close friends. She wasn't even close to Nick. It had been Nick who initiated contact with her. If she passed Nick in the hallway, it was he who spoke first. She had been so determined to get ahead in life, she hadn't taken the time to enjoy it.

She didn't go out with friends, and she didn't go to bars. She didn't do whatever people her age did. She'd had dates, but she didn't like anyone enough to stick around. Some had tried to get close, but she'd pushed them away. She had never gotten too close to people because they usually weren't around long enough to get close to. That had also applied to kids and foster parents. Kate sighed. She was so tired, she couldn't think straight.

Kate went through her nightly routine in a trance. She pulled back the covers on her bed and crawled in. She didn't think she would be able to sleep, but within minutes her eyelids grew heavy.

He was in the alley again, staying in the shadows. He looked up to see if he could get another glimpse of her. Tonight at the bookstore was better than he had hoped. She was truly an extraordinary woman. She had felt wonderful against him. It was as if they were made for each other. He was getting an erection again just thinking about it. Soon he wouldn't have to hide in the shadows. Kate would want to be with him. She would beg him to be with her. He smiled. They all begged in the end.

# 4

The next day Kate knocked at Nick's door. She waited, but still no answer came. *Where in the world is he?* It was early. He couldn't have left for work already. Maybe he had hooked up with someone. That was probably the case. She grabbed a pen and a paper out of her bag. She wrote a note telling him to get in contact with her as soon as possible. She folded the paper in half and slipped it under the door.

After that Kate went to the police station. She went to the officer behind the desk. He was a different person from the day before. *Was it only yesterday?* It felt like a lifetime ago. She asked for Detective Rowe. "What's your name?" he asked impatiently.

Kate didn't appreciate the tone, especially after the night she had had, but she told him anyway. The officer pushed a button on the phone, said something to whomever was on the other end, and set the phone back down. "Have a seat," he said rudely.

Kate waited for Detective Rowe, but it wasn't Rowe who came out. It was a guy a little older than Detective Rowe. He was handsome, about forty, and big. He looked as if he could be a linebacker for a professional football team. She wouldn't want to meet this guy in a dark alley.

He walked up to her and smiled. "Kate?"

She stood and had to tilt her head to look at him. She came only to his shoulders. "Where is Detective Rowe?" she asked.

"Detective Rowe was just put on another assignment. I'll be taking over your case." Kate frowned. "Come with me."

Kate followed him through the same gate as before, but this time they went down a hallway to a private office. The room wasn't large. It was just a desk with a couple chairs in front of it. A filing cabinet sat in the corner.

"Kate, I'm Detective Paine. You can call me Paine." He smiled. "People say I can be one sometimes." She chuckled and decided she liked him. "I'll be taking over your case. Unfortunately, I've had some experience with stalking cases before." Kate nodded. She didn't know what to say. "I've read the report about what happened last night, and I know you've done this already, but I would like to hear it from you again. Start at the beginning."

Kate took a deep breath and went through everything again—the feeling of being watched, the book she was reading, and the purple roses. She told him about the attack at the bookstore.

"And you don't have the roses?" he asked.

Kate sighed. "I left one at my neighbor's. I haven't been able to get it from him yet. The second rose I left outside my door. But when Detective Rowe and I went back to get it, it was gone."

"You don't have any idea who would do this to you? An ex-boyfriend or maybe an irate customer from the bookstore?"

"Detective Paine, if I knew who it was, don't you think I would have told you? I don't have any idea who it is," Kate said testily. She immediately regretted her words. "Look, I'm sorry, Detective Paine. I just don't know how to deal with this. I'm scared to go to class or work. It's been only a couple of days, but it feels like weeks."

"Please. Call me Paine." He smiled and didn't seem to have taken offense at her outburst. "I know it's scary and frustrating, but in most stalking cases, the most that ever happens are some notes or phone calls. I know this guy came into your workplace last night, but I think he just wanted to scare you."

*Well, it worked,* she thought. "What can you do to help me?"

Detective Paine ran a hand through his hair. "Normally, we would get a restraining order, but since we don't know who he is, we can't do that. We don't have the roses." Kate started to protest, but the detective cut her off. "But that doesn't mean we're not taking this seriously. We did dust for prints last night, but so many people go through that bookstore, it's going to be nearly impossible to get any help there. You can take some precautions, though. Try not to go anywhere alone," he said. Kate didn't know how that was going to work. She was almost always alone. "Keep your eyes open. Be aware of your surroundings. Do you have pepper spray?" Kate shook her head. "I know it doesn't sound like much, but it will help."

Kate still didn't understand why this was happening to her. She never bothered anyone. She minded her own business. She didn't do anything to draw attention to herself. She just wanted to finish school and move on. Lost in thought, Kate didn't realize the detective had gotten up and was waiting for her. Kate stood on wobbly legs.

"Kate, here's my card with my cell number on it. Program it into your phone. If for any reason you feel scared or threatened, call me, and I'll be there."

Kate took the card and nodded. "Thank you, Detective Paine." Kate stopped and smiled shyly. "I mean, thank you, Paine."

"That's better," he said warmly.

Paine watched her go. She was a nice kid. He wondered why there were so many assholes out there. Sometimes he really hated his job. He had dealt with many things in his career, but when a man hurt or threatened a woman, it set his teeth on edge. He was going to do everything he could to help her. He picked up the phone and dialed.

After Kate left the police station, she headed for work. Her shift hadn't started yet, but she didn't want to go home. She thought about what the detective had said, and looked around at her surroundings as she walked. She didn't feel any eyes on her or see anyone paying any attention to her. She hated always being afraid somebody was going to jump out at her. She couldn't let this man control her life. She was stronger than this. She'd taken care of herself for most of her life. This was just another stumbling block.

She arrived at the bookstore without incident. She stowed her belongings in the back room and went to find Mags. She was going to have to ask for shifts where she never worked alone. Kate hated asking for any kind of special treatment, but she wasn't going to take any risk.

This guy would either get bored and move on, or the police would find out who he was. Kate hoped, anyway.

She found Mags in the children's section of the bookstore. Mags looked up and saw Kate. She put the book she was holding down and rushed over to give Kate a big hug. "Oh, honey, how are you doing?"

"I'm okay." Kate fought back the tears. "But I need to talk to you about my schedule. I hate asking you this, but I was wondering if I could work only when there are at least two of us here."

Mags patted her hand. "Honey, it's quite all right. Of course we can do that. I just have to change a few things around. What about your school schedule, though?"

"I've already made an appointment with my professor for tomorrow. I'm going to see about changing my night classes." Kate didn't want to talk to the professor either, but she didn't see she had any choice. Until this was over, she was going to be very cautious.

"If you ever need anything, you can always call me," Mags said with concern.

Kate gave her a hug. "Thank you for understanding." *If nothing else,* Kate thought, *I'm becoming quite the hugger from this experience.*

Kate was surprised how quickly the day went. She didn't think about her stalker too much, but she still thought about him more than she wanted to. Mags stayed with her until closing, which Kate appreciated. They were closing up when Kate told Mags she appreciated her staying longer than she normally would.

"Honey, I got caught up on a whole lot of paperwork. It was nothing to stay. I'm not going to let anything happen to you."

Kate felt the tears again, but she held them back. She was turning into a regular crybaby. After Mags locked the door, she turned to Kate. "How about I walk you home?"

"Thank you, Mags, but it's not that far, and the street is still pretty busy. I'll be okay."

"At least text me when you get home."

Kate promised she would, and they went their separate ways. When Kate arrived at home, she immediately went to Nick's door. She knocked and waited. After getting no answer, she knocked harder.

Kate was starting to get worried. Where was Nick? She wondered if she should call the police. She didn't know if he had family, and she didn't know any of his friends. He was a good neighbor and friend, but she didn't know anything about him. She did know where he worked, though. She could go to the bar and see if he was there. She would have to take the bus to get there. Just the thought of getting on it made her cringe. She told herself she could do this. There were always people on the bus, and the bus stop wasn't that far from the bar. She kept repeating to herself that she could do this. Having made the decision, she headed out again. She saw the bus coming and ran to the stop. After getting on, she looked around. She didn't see anything except people minding their own business. It was just people going home after a long day of work, or some going to work. She didn't see anything to cause her any concern.

Once she arrived at the stop for the bar, she hopped off. Luckily, the bar wasn't too far from the bus stop. She kept looking around. Still nothing seemed out of the ordinary. She was almost to the bar when she heard music coming out onto the street. Bars were not Kate's thing, but she had heard other students talking about all the different ones they would visit and about all the different guys in those bars. It seemed normal to Kate that they wanted to go to bars. So why didn't she? Granted, she was usually older than most of the other students in her classes, but not by much.

Approaching the door, she opened it and went in. It took a few moments for her eyes to adjust to the room's dimness. It was very busy and loud. She worked her way through the crowd and toward the counter where a couple of guys were making drinks. She noticed guys looking at her, and some even tried to talk to her, but she ignored them. She just wanted to find out about Nick and get out of there.

She stepped up to the counter. "Excuse me," she said to the guy closest to her. She waited for him to look her way. He was in his early thirties with longer hair swept across his forehead. He turned toward her with a questioning look. "Can you tell me if Nick is working tonight?"

She had to yell to be heard over the music. He was looking her up and down. Kate didn't know if he was checking her out or trying to decide if she was an ex-girlfriend coming to cause trouble.

"I'm his neighbor," she said. He just kept looking at her. "I haven't seen him for a few days, and I'm worried about him."

He seemed to come to a decision. "Nick hasn't been here since his shift two nights ago. He was scheduled to work last night and tonight. That's why I'm here." He sounded annoyed. "So, if you see him, tell him he owes me big time."

A customer drew his attention, and the bartender turned away to help. Kate stepped back from the counter and bumped into some-body. She turned to apologize, but the person had already moved away. She only caught a glimpse of the back of a head. She stood there thinking about Nick. He was a responsible guy. He didn't miss work. He couldn't afford to. So where was he? After getting bumped again, Kate decided it was time to leave. Weaving through the crowd, she was jostled and mauled. She remembered why she didn't go to bars. She had just reached the door when somebody grabbed her from behind. "Hey, sweet thing. Where are you going?" His words were slurred.

*Great. Now I have to deal with a drunk.* Kate turned and gave him a dirty look. He didn't take the hint. He took hold of her arm again. "Come on, honey. Let me buy you a drink."

She tried jerking her arm loose, but he wouldn't let go. He was starting to hurt her. "Look, buddy, I don't want a drink, so could you please let go of my arm?"

He squeezed her harder. Kate pushed his chest firmly with her other arm. He stumbled back and glared at her. "Bitch, you think you're too good to have a drink with me?" the man snarled.

Kate didn't respond. She turned, walked out the door, and rushed to the bus stop. Her heart was pounding. Going to the bar had defi-nitely been a mistake. Nick wasn't there, and now she would probably have bruises on her arm. All in all it was not a good night. When the bus came, she hopped on and went home.

He watched them from across the bar. The bastard was grabbing Kate's arm. Nobody touched her like that. Clenching his fists, he started toward them. Anger reddened his face. She was his. He stopped when he saw Kate push the bastard. The man almost fell. He snickered. It served him right. He saw Kate leave, and he watched the guy as he moved back toward the bar.

Inside the bar, he walked up to the drunk man. "Tough night, huh?" he said sympathetically.

The guy turned his bloodshot eyes toward him. "The bitch wouldn't even let me buy her a drink. She thought she was too good for anybody in this room."

"Maybe you shouldn't have called her a bitch," he said in a cold voice.

The guy scowled. "Hey, buddy, I don't think it's any of your business. So, why don't you go back to whatever hole you crawled out of and stay there?"

The bastard turned away and headed back toward the counter to get another drink. *That's right, asshole. You keep drinking, and I'll see you later.* He smiled. This was going to be fun. He left remembering the way Kate had felt against him.

# 5

The next couple of days went by without any incident. Kate still kept a watchful eye on her surroundings. She talked to her professor and arranged for different classes. Kate didn't explain, and he didn't ask. It would probably stop her from finishing the semester on time, but Kate didn't care. She just wanted to feel safe.

There was still no sign of Nick. She called Detective Paine and told him she was worried about him. The detective said he would look into it.

She was never alone at the bookstore. Mags always kept a close eye on her. On the fifth day without incident (that was how Kate counted her days now), Detective Paine came in. Kate had just finished with a customer when she saw him. She knew immediately something was wrong.

"Hi, Kate. Can we go somewhere and talk?"

"Um, sure." On shaky legs she took him to the back room of the bookstore. She knew this couldn't be good. Her heart was pounding so hard, she was sure Paine could hear it. When they were in the back room, she turned to him.

"Kate, maybe you should sit down."

The back room wasn't that big. There was a desk with a filing cabinet, and across from it was a counter with a coffeepot on top and a small refrigerator underneath it. Paine took up the rest of the available space. She sat on the edge of the desk. She didn't think she could stand much longer. Her legs felt like noodles.

The detective reached into his jacket and brought out a photo. "Do you know this guy?" he asked.

Kate took the photo and looked at it. At first glance she didn't know him, but then she remembered. "This guy was at the bar where Nick works. He wanted to buy me a drink, and I told him no." She handed the photo back to him. "I don't know what he has to do..." Kate stood up abruptly. "Wait, is this my stalker? You caught him?" She felt such relief, she had to sit back down on the desk.

"Kate." He was shaking his head and staring at her with concern. "This isn't your stalker."

Her heart sank. "What does he have to do with anything then? I don't understand."

The detective stepped toward her and set his hand on her shoulder. "He was found earlier this morning. Dead." He was looking at her closely. "His throat was cut."

All the color drained from Kate's face. She started shaking. This couldn't possibly have anything to do with her. She told Paine that.

"He was found in an alley two buildings down from the bar where Nick works."

"That still doesn't mean it has anything to do with me," she said desperately. She couldn't help it.

"He was found with a note on his chest." The detective paused but still watched her closely. She felt like a bug under a microscope.

Kate couldn't stand it. "Please just say whatever it is you have to say."

"The note said, 'Kate, do you notice me yet?' There was a purple rose lying with the note."

Kate couldn't breathe. She needed air. She tried to rise, but the detective put his arm around her shoulders. "Kate, listen to me."

She shrugged his shoulder away, not hearing him. All she could see was the guy at the bar. Then another thought occurred to her. "He was there. My stalker was there that night."

"Kate, look at me."

*Oh God, I'm going to be sick.* She ran out of the back room and into the restroom. She barely made it to the sink before she threw up everything she had eaten that day. When she didn't have anything left in her stomach, she reached for a paper towel. She turned on the faucet and put the towel underneath it. She lifted her head and looked at herself in the mirror. Her face was void of all color. She looked like death.

There was a knock on the door, and the detective walked in. He looked at her sympathetically. He took the paper towel from her hand and started wiping her face.

"I can do it," she said, and took it back from him. Kate finished wiping her face and then rinsed her mouth with water. Detective Paine didn't say anything. He just watched her. Once she was done, she turned to him. "Now what?" Her voice was scratchy.

"Now we have to talk about the night at the bar." He put his hand on her shoulder gently. "When you're ready, we'll go back to the office."

Kate wasn't sure if she could talk about it now. She knew she didn't have a choice, though, if she ever wanted to get her life back.

When they were in the office again, she turned to him. "Did you ever find out anything about Nick?"

The detective crossed his arms. "We checked out his apartment. Everything looked fine. Nothing was disturbed. His clothes all seemed to be there, so it doesn't look as if he went on a trip. We talked to both of his bosses, and he hasn't been to work at either place since last week. They both said it wasn't like him to miss work."

Kate's thoughts were swirling. She knew in her gut something had happened to Nick.

"We're treating it as a missing person case now."

"What about his family?" Kate again wished she had asked Nick more about his relatives.

"We haven't been able to find any family. But we'll keep at it, Kate. We'll find him."

Kate nodded absently. She couldn't stop thinking that if she knew more about Nick's life, she could help find him.

"Kate?"

She realized the detective must have asked her something. "What?"

"I was asking if you were ready to talk about the other night. At the bar."

*No,* she thought. Instead she nodded. "What do you want to know?"

The detective moved a little closer. He probably thought she was going to faint. "Just tell me what happened. Step by step."

Taking a deep breath, Kate started her story. She told him about taking the bus to the bar and asking the bartender about Nick. She told him about trying to get out of the bar when the man grabbed her arm. "What's his—" Kate cleared her throat. "What was his name?" She thought she should at least know his name.

"Kate, this isn't your fault. It's the asshole's fault who killed him. He's a sick bastard. In his twisted mind he probably thought he was making a gallant gesture. To impress you."

Kate heard him and even understood, but she couldn't help how she felt. "What was his name?"

The detective sighed. "Don Sherman. He was an accountant at a firm downtown. He wasn't married, and he had no kids."

*Well, that's something at least,* Kate thought. *No kids.* She didn't know what she would do if kids were involved.

"Let's go back to that night. Do you remember anything else? Anything that seemed odd or out of place?"

Kate thought about that night. She went over it in her head. "It wasn't even that odd, but I guess the only other thing was that I bumped into somebody after I spoke to the bartender. I turned to apologize, but he was gone." She looked at the detective. "The bar was crowded, though. I bumped into a lot of people."

The detective nodded. "Could you describe him?"

"No. He was gone when I turned around."

"Are you sure it was a man?"

Kate looked at the detective and frowned. "I saw only the back of his head, but he seemed to be taller than I am. I'm pretty sure it was a man. Do you think it was him?"

"I don't know, Kate. I'm just trying to get a handle on this thing." He moved toward the door. His back was to her.

"Are the police going to be able to help me?" she asked. Her voice was wobbly. She thought she was going to lose it again. *They don't know anything about this guy. They don't know what he looks like. How do you look for a ghost?*

The detective turned back to her. His eyes were angry, but she knew that anger wasn't directed at her. "Kate, we're going to get this guy. I promise, I won't let anything happen to you. But I need you to be cautious. Don't go anywhere alone. No more visiting bars." Paine said meaningfully. "Be aware. Did you get your pepper spray?"

Kate nodded. She didn't know if pepper spray would stop this guy, but it did make her feel a little better. She was thinking about getting a gun when she heard the detective talking. "I'm going to have somebody outside your apartment. We'll be there with you at work. Don't take the bus anymore. If it's not within walking distance, you don't go there. We can keep a better eye on you when you're walking."

Kate was shaking her head. "I have to take the bus for school. I don't have a car. I have to finish school. I'm almost done," she said with frustration. This guy was destroying the life she had worked so hard to get. She wondered again why this was happening to her. It didn't make any sense.

"Kate, I understand how hard this is for you. But we will catch this guy, and then you can get your life back. Until then you have to be careful. You can go to work, but I'm sorry, Kate, no school." Kate started to protest, but the detective continued. "Hopefully, it won't be long." He stepped in front of her. "It's not worth risking your life for. This guy has already killed once."

Kate wanted to throw something. She was going to have to quit or at least postpone school. She knew she couldn't stop and then pick up where she had left off. It didn't work that way. She would have to take the whole semester over again if she couldn't talk the professor into letting her doing it remotely. Then she remembered the man who had been killed. Kate felt ashamed. At least she was still alive. Kate didn't say anything more. She just nodded.

"I'm going to introduce you to three of my detectives. There will be only three. No one else. If you see anybody else following you, or even feel as if someone is following you, I want you to tell the detectives. They will get you somewhere safe, and we'll take care of the rest." Not waiting for a response, he took her arm and led Kate out of the office. "Let's go talk to your boss. I'm going to take you to the station and introduce you to those detectives."

They arrived at the station, and Paine steered her into the same office as before. The noise of the station faded when he shut the door. She was grateful. Kate wasn't sure how much more she could take.

*God bless Mags,* Kate thought. When she had told her what was going on, Mags just hugged Kate and told her to do whatever was necessary.

"I'll be right back, Kate."

He left her alone, and she felt a moment of panic. *You're safe, Kate. You're in a police station for Pete's sake.* She still felt a little nervous by herself, and she wondered what she was going to do alone in her apartment that night. Trying to take her mind off it, she took a seat. She took her phone out of her bag and was looking up her school schedule when Paine walked back in.

Three men came in behind him. They were all looking at her. Feeling self-conscious, Kate pushed her hair behind her ear. They were all tall, well built, and handsome. *They all must drink from the same well,* Kate thought.

Paine started the introductions. "Kate, these are Detectives Jones, Marsh, and Hansen."

The three detectives stepped forward.

"Ma'am, I'm Ben Jones." Kate shook his hand. He was the tallest of the four men. He had dark hair and dark green eyes. She guessed he was in his late thirties.

The next man came forward. "I'm Jake Marsh. The best-looking one," he said with a twinkle in his eyes. Kate smiled back. He was very handsome. He had long blond hair and light blue eyes. Kate thought he should be on a beach somewhere waiting to catch the next wave. She put him in his late twenties.

Then the last detective stepped up. "I'm Bill Hansen," he said quietly. He was the oldest of the three—maybe mid-forties. He gave her a small smile. He had short light reddish hair with a sprinkle of freckles across his nose. The nose looked as if it had been broken at one time. Kate couldn't tell what color his eyes were. He didn't look at her long enough. He might have been the oldest, but he was just as muscular as the rest.

When the introductions were done, Paine walked around his desk and sat down. "Kate, these are the men I assigned to look out for you. You will never be alone. One of these guys will always be around. Even if you can't see them, they will be there."

Kate sat down. She knew her life was definitely going to be different.

"We're going to try to stay out of your way. We want you to go about your life as normal. Except school, of course," Paine said.

Kate tried to smile, but she faltered. How could she go about her life when there was a guy out there willing to kill just because someone gave her a hard time? It was insane.

"I'm not sure how all this is going to work," she said to Paine. "These men have their own lives. They can't be with me constantly."

Detective Hansen came forward. "Kate. Is it all right if I call you Kate?"

Kate nodded. "Of course."

He gave her another small smile. "Kate, we all know what this is going to take." He looked around at the other men. "But we're in this with you. We all volunteered for this. It's our job, but mostly, we just don't like men who threaten women."

"Besides, you're so pretty. You'll be doing us the favor," the beach hunk said with the same twinkle as before.

Kate looked around at the men. She didn't know what kind of emotion she should feel for them. She had only just met them, yet these men were willing to give up so much to help her. She looked down at her lap. She had to blink several times to clear her eyes. She was not going to cry in front of them.

The room was very quiet. Paine cleared his throat. "Okay, Kate. Let's get you home. If one of these guys can't be with you, I'll step in. Mostly, though, I'll be working the case from here."

Kate stood. Not caring what they thought, she gave each man a hug. "So, who's with me first?"

Jake stepped up. "That would be me, darlin'."

Bending his elbow and turning it toward her, Kate put her arm through his. *Here we go,* she thought.

6

He had watched the guy for a couple of days. It had meant he couldn't keep his eye on Kate, but this couldn't be helped. The stupid bastard hadn't even known he'd been on his tail. And when the asshole had stepped into the alley, he couldn't believe his luck.

That night he'd looked around to make sure there'd been no prying eyes. He'd followed him into the alley. He'd found the guy urinating on a wall. He'd been drunk again, so he hadn't heard him step up behind him. "You should learn to keep your hands to yourself."

Before the man could react, he'd slit his throat. He'd fallen where he'd stood. Then he'd placed the note and the rose on his chest and left. All that had taken under five minutes. It'd been so damn easy.

Now he was standing outside the police station. He wondered if she appreciated what he had done for her. That guy would never bother her again. *What is taking her so long?* he thought. He wanted to see her face, see if she was as excited as he was. The only disappointing part of the night was that he hadn't gotten to beat the shit out of the guy. It hadn't been a challenge.

He saw the police station door open. *There! There she is. She's beautiful.* He saw the guy holding the door open for her. *Who's this?* He continued to watch. They headed down the street, the man's hand resting on her back. He was struggling to control his anger. *Is this how she says thank you?* He knew the guy was a cop and a damn cocky one too. He started to follow them. *So, she has protection now.* All his anger instantly vanished when a new feeling came over him. He smiled. *At last. A challenge.*

A different life began for Kate that day. She was never left alone. Even at night the police were out there protecting her. Sometimes she would make the detectives come in for a bite to eat. It was the least she could do.

Little by little she learned things about each of them. She was going to do things different this time. She wanted to get to know these men. Paine was the only married one. The rest were single, which surprised Kate. They were all charming in different ways. Bill rarely talked, but she could tell even he was warming up to her. She asked Bill once why he had never married.

"I was married once. She died five years ago." Kate didn't know what to say to that. "You know that old cliché about being married to our jobs? It would take a special woman to put up with that. And I already had my special woman."

Kate had to swallow the lump in her throat. He looked so sad. Thankfully, Bill smiled and broke the dark mood.

She also learned Ben had had a fiancée. She asked what had happened.

"I don't know. I guess I wasn't there enough. I came home from work early one day." His jaw clenched. "She was with some guy from her office."

"What did you do?" she asked.

"I packed up and left."

Kate gave him a hug. "She was crazy, Ben. You're a great guy who deserves better than that."

Embarrassed, Ben stepped away. "So now I have trust issues," he said jokingly.

Then there was Jake. He continually flirted with her, but she knew it didn't mean anything. She had once told him to find a girl and go out on a date. He had laughed. "Darlin', you're the only girl for me." Then he had grown serious. "Honestly, though. Right now, Kate, you are the only girl I need to worry about." Kate did cry that time.

Kate went to work and tried to be normal. Whenever she helped male customers, she always looked at them longer than she should. She looked to see if she saw anything sinister in their eyes, but she never got a bad vibe off anybody. Sometimes, though, the customers looked at her as if she were the problem.

Days turned into weeks, and weeks turned into months. Two months later nothing had happened. Kate didn't know which was worse—waiting for something to happen or nothing happening at all. There was still nothing on Nick. He had just disappeared.

Paine checked in with her at least once a week. She would have him over for dinner too. One night he was unusually quiet. She asked him what was wrong. He told her he had separated from his wife. This upset Kate. Paine was such a sweet, caring man. She didn't understand why a woman would give up a man like Paine. Kate laid her hand over his. "Why?"

He made the same comment as Bill about it being too hard to be married to a cop. Kate could tell he still loved his wife, though. His eyes would light up whenever he talked about her.

The reports he gave about her stalker were always the same—nothing new. They had no new leads to follow, and Paine confessed he wasn't sure what to do at this point.

At the end of the second month, Kate rushed home from work. She was going to fix dinner for Jake and Paine tonight. She enjoyed the company. Having been alone most of her life, she hadn't known what she was missing. These guys had become her family. She almost forgot they were cops protecting her. They treated her like family too. She was like a sister. She knew she would continue to see them after everything was over. She couldn't imagine not having them in her life.

They were at the end of the meal when she turned to Paine. "How much longer can you guys keep protecting me?" Paine just looked at her. "Come on. You and I know this can't continue. Nothing has happened for two months. Maybe he's given up," she said hopefully.

Jake spoke first. "We're not going to leave you unprotected."

"Jake, I know you don't want to, but let me ask you a question. When was your last date?"

"I told you, Kate. For now you're it."

"You guys can't keep this up. I'm surprised the department has even let it go on this long." They both looked away. "Okay, guys. What's up?" Jake still couldn't seem to look at her, so she turned her attention to Paine instead. "Paine?"

He was running his hand through his hair. She knew what that meant. When he finally looked at her, she knew. He didn't have to say it. Time was up.

"How long do we have?" Kate asked.

She kept her face neutral. These men had given up so much for her. She would not make them feel any worse, even if her heart felt as if it were going to pound out of her chest.

"We have another week. If I can't find a new lead or if something doesn't happen within that time, they're pulling us."

Kate stood and walked into the living room. They followed her. Jake walked over to her and pulled her in for a hug. "We're still going to keep protecting you. We'll be here on our days off and after our shifts. We can still make it work so somebody is always with you."

Kate hugged him back, but after a moment she pulled away. "I'm not going to ask you guys to do that."

"Who said you had to ask? We're doing it. Period," he said angrily. She looked at him with affection. "We're family now, and that's the way it's going to be."

Kate took his hands in hers. "I don't want you to do it. I want all of you to get back to your lives and go out on dates. I want you to work things out with your wife," she said to Paine. "It's been two months. He's given up. It doesn't mean I still won't be cautious. I'll be aware." She smiled at Paine.

"You can forget it, Kate. It's not happening. All of us have already worked this out. We're doing it."

"For how long?" Her voice rose. "It's not possible. I won't allow it. I have to get my life back too. If I let this continue, he wins." Both Paine and Jake started to talk at the same time, but Kate held up her hand to cut them off. "No. This is how it's going to go. Who's the best shot of all of you?"

Paine grabbed her arm but not hard enough to hurt. It did get her attention, though. "Why? Now you want to get a gun?" he asked harshly.

"Yes, and I want you all to teach me to shoot it."

They were all very good shots, but they kept arguing among themselves about who was best, and they took turns taking her to the shooting range. She learned something different from each of them. They all decided a .22-caliber Sig Sauer Mosquito was the right gun for her. It was light, and its recoil was minimal.

They taught her how to hold the gun with two hands and how to set her legs and arms. She always felt as if she were on a TV show, hunting down a suspect. They taught her how to take the gun apart and clean it. She practiced taking it apart before and after they went to the shooting range. By the end of the week, Kate was feeling comfortable with the gun. She wasn't the best shot, but she was getting better. Paine had helped with the concealed weapon permit. He told her to carry it with her too. Now she was ready. She hoped.

She decided on the last night of her protection to make dinner for them all. She knew they weren't happy with the situation, but she kept refusing when they tried to talk her into changing her mind. They were all sitting around her table. There wasn't much conversation. Everyone seemed lost in their own thoughts.

"Come on, guys. This is supposed to be a fun night. You guys look as if you're waiting for the firing squad."

Ben pushed back from the table and knocked his chair over. Kate jumped. "Kate, this isn't a celebration dinner." His voice shook with anger. "Do you really think we can just leave you alone, unprotected?"

Kate stood. "Ben, I know it's not. I'm well aware of what the situation is. I can't think about *him* all the time, though. I'd go crazy. I will remain aware and careful."

Bill stood too. "Kate." He spoke calmly and gave Ben a dirty look. "What the dick wad over there is trying to say is we will always be here for you. We know you want to get your life back, and we want that too. You have to know, though, even though we won't be here every second of the day, we will be here when we can. All of us."

Jake piped in. "So you're just going to have deal with it."

Tears ran down her cheeks. She wondered how she had gotten lucky enough for these men to come into her life. Then she thought, it was strange that she never would have met them if she weren't being stalked.

"Ah hell, Kate. Don't cry." Jake came over and put his arms around her. "Way to go, asshole," he said to Ben. "You made her cry."

Ben started sputtering, and Kate laughed at his expression. "Ben, you didn't make me cry." Ben smiled at her and then gave Jake the same dirty look. "You guys have become so important to me, and I'm just going to miss not having you around all the time."

"Be careful what you wish for," Paine said. "You might get sick of us and never want to talk to us again when this is over."

"I doubt that," Kate said, and wiped tears from her eyes. She gave each man a small smile. "Now, who wants dessert?"

Kate lay in her bed the next morning. This was her first day alone. She would never have told the guys, but she was scared. She tried to tell herself her stalker had given up. He had gotten bored and moved on when he couldn't get to her. She meant moved on, period, rather than moved on to somebody else. She wouldn't wish that on her worst enemy. "Come on, Kate. You can do this." *Great. I'm talking to myself again.*

She had stalled as long as possible. Kate pushed back the covers and got up. She went through her morning routine of brushing her teeth and combing her hair. Kate knew her greatest asset was her hair. After that night in the bookstore, she had considered cutting it, but she thought that would have given her stalker a win. So she'd kept it long. She would normally have fixed herself something to eat, but the thought of food made her stomach churn. She gathered her stuff for work. Fortunately, the professor had let her keep up on her assignments so she wouldn't have to take the whole semester over. It will be nice to be actually in the classroom again though. After making sure her gun and pepper spray were in her bag, she took a deep breath and left her apartment.

Once outside, she stopped and looked around. She stood, looking for a couple of minutes, trying to be aware of her surroundings. Not seeing anything out of the ordinary, she took off toward work. *Everything's fine,* she told herself. *There's nobody here.* She was sure she would feel someone's presence. She had before. She couldn't help how relieved she felt when she arrived at work. It was only the first day, and she felt like she was going to have a heart attack. She had to calm down or she wouldn't make it to day two.

Mags came over to her. "Hi, honey. I need you to help set up the new section of the children's area. All the new books came in."

The renovated children's section was more of a teen section. Mags had changed the room around so teens would have more separation. She said teenagers had it hard enough, and they could make them feel a little special. Mags had put in iPads and had had them bolted to the desks. "They're special, but let's not tempt them." She also had bean-bags and stuffed chairs lying around the room, as well as one couch. The colors were bright and cheery.

Kate would listen to some of the kids' conversations. She didn't think it was eavesdropping if they were talking loud enough for her to hear.

She noticed one kid in particular. He was about sixteen and had light brown hair and the greenest eyes she had ever seen. He was a good-looking kid. She noticed the high school girls looking at him too. She had to smile, because he didn't seem to notice. He'd been coming in for a couple of months now, and he always started a conversation with Kate. She knew he had a crush on her, but it was harmless. She eventually learned his name was Tyler, and he went to a nearby high school. Tyler had approached Kate one day when Ben was on her guard. Ben had put his hand on Tyler's shoulder. "You need something, kid?" Tyler had swallowed hard and told Ben he was looking for a book and was asking Kate for help. Kate smiled and tried to hide her amusement because she had no idea what book she could supposedly find for Tyler.

Kate was still working in the teen section when Tyler came in. As usual, he went over to her. "Hi, Kate."

"Hey, Tyler. How was school?"

"It was all right. The same old boring stuff. What are you doing?"

Kate looked at him and smiled. "I'm putting these new books away. You should check some of them out. I think you would like a couple of them."

Tyler shrugged. "Maybe."

Kate looked at him again. Seeing his expression, she put the book down that she was holding. "Okay. What's up? You look as if you just lost your best friend." Tyler wouldn't meet her eyes. "Tyler, what is it?" Kate asked with concern.

He finally looked at her. "I notice you don't have somebody with you today." Kate just looked at him. "I mean, you always seem to have someone with you. Watching you. Like a bodyguard or something."

*Wow. This kid is good. If he noticed, did anybody else?* Kate looked around the store. She didn't see anyone staring at her. *There's nobody there. Get a grip, Kate. You're probably scaring the kid.*

She turned back to look at him. She saw the concern on his young face. Kate felt touched. "It's okay, Tyler. Everything's fine. I had some trouble several months ago, and they were watching out for me. But it's all good now." *I hope.*

"What kind of trouble?" Tyler asked.

"Nothing you need to worry about." She saw the hurt expression on his face. *Way to go, Kate. Now you hurt the kid's feelings.* "It was somebody who wouldn't leave me alone. But it's over now."

"Did they catch him?"

Kate sighed. She wondered how she'd gotten into this conversation. She smiled at him. "It's all over now, so you don't have to worry about me. Okay?"

Tyler looked at her, and after a moment he nodded. "Can I help you do anything?" he asked.

Kate thanked him, told him no, and recommended some books for him to read. To her great relief, that seemed to distract him. He started telling her about the kinds of books he liked.

The rest of the afternoon went pretty quickly. The teen section took up most of Kate's day, and she was grateful for the distraction. She was just finishing up when Mags came over to her. "Hey, honey. Thanks so much for doing this for me."

"It was great. I liked doing it. It's fun to see new books come in. I kind of browsed through some of them. Might have to read some myself." Kate smiled.

Kate was startled when Mags grabbed her hands. "How are you doing? I noticed your people weren't here today."

*Jeez. Did everybody know?* "You noticed too?" Kate asked.

"Honey, I would have to be dead not to notice those boys. Every single one of them was a manly man. If I were a few years younger…"

Kate was dumbfounded. Then she burst into laughter.

Mags turned serious again. "I mean it, honey. What's going on? I know they didn't catch the guy, so what gives? Where are your boys?"

Kate squeezed Mags's hands and let go. "No. They didn't catch him. It has been months, though, and nothing else has happened. We knew this couldn't go on forever."

"So they just left you alone?" Mags said incredulously.

Kate reached for her hands again. "They didn't want to go, but they didn't have a choice. Besides, I told them to go. It was time. I need my life back. Tomorrow I'm going to the school to enroll again. Then I'm just taking it one day at a time."

Mags gave her a hug. "I don't like this. I don't like it one little bit. They're the police. They should protect you."

Kate hugged her back. "It's okay, Mags. Everything will be fine. My boys told me they'll still be around. Maybe not every second, but as much as they can." Kate heard Mags sniff, and pulled away to look at her. "Mags, look at me. I promise it's okay. I'm scared, but I can handle this, and so can you. We'll do this together. Okay?"

Mags nodded, gave her another hug, and pulled away. Embarrassed by her crying, she started fussing with the rest of the books. "Okay. Let's get this cleaned, and then we can lock up."

Once they'd gotten everything picked up, Kate got her stuff from the back room. She met Mags at the front door. "Ready?" Mags asked.

"I'm ready," she said, trying to convince Mags as much as herself. They opened the door and turned so Mags could lock up. Kate was searching through her purse when she realized she didn't have her keys or pepper spray. She figured they must have fallen out into her cubbyhole. "Wait, Mags. I don't have my keys. I have to go get them."

"Okay. I'll wait here for you."

"No. It's not necessary. I can do this. I've got to do it sometime. And it's Monday. I know you have an appointment."

Mags was shaking her head. "It will wait."

Kate patted her hand. "Mags, I appreciate it. Really, I do, but you need to go. I *can* do this." Mags wavered. She was clearly not happy with the situation. "Go. I'll be fine," Kate said.

Mags huffed out a breath. "Okay, I'll go, but I want you to call me as soon as you get home. I mean it, Kate. As soon as you get home."

Kate smiled and held up three fingers for the Girl Scout salute. "I promise."

"Okay then. I'll see you tomorrow." Mags smiled, turned, and left.

Kate stood at the door and looked around. Mustering all the courage she could, she stepped back into the store. She locked the door behind her. She wasn't taking any chances. She reached out, turned on the light switch, and headed for the back room. She found her keys in the cubbyhole. She wasn't sure how they could have fallen out. She would have to be more careful. She was heading back to the door when the lights went out.

# 7

**P**aine was just finishing up some paperwork when Bill came into his office. "Hey, Bill. You all done for the day?"

Bill sat down in the chair in front of Paine's desk. "Yep. Just wanted to check in and see if you had anything new to report."

Paine leaned back in his chair and ran a hand through his hair. He figured he'd be bald before this case was over. "I have nothing. I can't seem to get a handle on this. How does a guy stalk a woman, kill a man as if he's doing her some fucking favor, and then disappear? He left no evidence at the crime scene. No prints at her apartment. Nothing. Then he leaves her alone for two months. It's almost as if he knows about our investigation. Our schedules."

Bill was frowning at him. "What are you saying?"

Paine leaned forward in his chair. "Think about it. He leaves no evidence, which is not unheard of, but when you put that with us being there for months and nothing happening, it's almost as if he's one step ahead of us. It just doesn't add up."

Bill stood and started pacing. He stopped in front of the desk. "You think it's a cop." He said it as a statement rather than a question.

"I don't know what I'm saying. I just know I'm frustrated as hell."

Bill started pacing again. "He could have seen us with Kate. It's not as if we tried to hide it. Hell, isn't that what we wanted? Him to know we were there?"

"I know. You're right. There's something in my gut, though, telling me he's a cop."

Bill kept pacing. "A cop would have information about the case and our surveillance. He could pretty much find out anything he needed to know." Bill said this more to himself than to Paine.

"Can you please sit the fuck down? You're driving me crazy!" Paine yelled, and ran his hand through his hair again. Bill stopped and looked at Paine. "I'm sorry, Bill. This case is going to be the death of me. Nobody should have to go through what Kate's going through."

Bill sat down. "I know, Paine. We all feel the same way about her. She's a special lady. But it's hard to think this is a cop." Bill took a deep breath. "I think you're right, though. It makes the most sense."

Paine set his hands on his desk and laced his fingers. "Let's assume for a minute it is a cop." Bill nodded. "He would have to be somebody from this precinct. He would have known who was with Kate and when."

Bill nodded. "Which was all the time. He knew he couldn't make a move with one of us there. That means we probably know him and would recognize him."

"Right," Paine said, and ran his hand through his hair again. He was going to have to stop that if he wanted any hair left at all. "Let's assume we're right. We need to talk to Ben and Jake and fill them in. We can't trust anybody but us."

Bill nodded but didn't say anything. Paine saw Bill get up and start pacing again. Paine couldn't blame him. He felt like doing the same thing. Instead Paine picked up the phone on his desk. Paine talked to both Ben and Jake and told them his theory. Surprisingly, they both seemed to agree. They all seemed to be on the same page. Paine had just put the phone back when Bill stopped suddenly. "I'm going over to Kate's now. I've got a bad feeling."

Paine stood. "I'll go with you."

Paine didn't want to admit it to Bill, but he also had a bad feeling. They both left the station in a hurry.

Kate stood frozen. *No, no, no. Not again.* She could feel him behind her. She didn't want to turn to face him. Tears came to her eyes. *Why did I let Mags leave? I'm not ready for this. I thought I was strong, but I'm not.* Kate started shaking when he put his hand on her shoulder. He whispered in her ear. "Kate, I've waited so long to touch you again." She tried to hide the gag reflex that hit her. "I've missed you. Did you miss me?"

She could smell his breath's stench. He squeezed her shoulder harder. Kate winced in pain. "Did you miss me?" he asked louder.

"Yes," Kate choked out. She hoped if she went along with whatever he said, he wouldn't hurt her.

"I've waited for you. I've waited to touch you and for you to notice me. I know it's not your fault those cops wouldn't leave you alone."

*Think, Kate. Can I get into my bag? Can I get my pepper spray?* Then she remembered her pepper spray wasn't in her bag. *Where's my gun? Is it in my bag? How could you forget to check for your gun?* She was praying it was still in there. She was waiting to make her move when he stepped back from her. "Kate, I want you to turn around and move to the back room."

*This could be my chance. I have to get my gun out of my bag.* Kate was afraid to move any part of her body. *You can do this, Kate. You have to do it. You have to save yourself.* As she was turning to go to the back room, he turned with her and stayed behind her. She still hadn't seen his face. Maybe that was a good sign.

"Did you like my surprises?" he asked.

Kate started moving the bag in front of her very slowly. She hoped he wouldn't see it. Her hopes fell as he reached around and grabbed it. She tried to hang on to it, but he yanked it out of her hands. "Now, Kate, what could you have in your bag?" He snickered. "Your gun is not in there, Kate. I removed it earlier, along with your keys."

Kate's heart sank. He had taken her gun. *How could I have not noticed my gun was missing? Now what? I still need a distraction.*

"Someday, Kate, you'll learn you can't outsmart me," he said as he turned her bag upside down and dumped its contents onto the floor.

*Maybe while he's distracted, I can push him and run for the door.*

"What's this?" he said, and bent down.

*This is it, Kate. It's now or never. Move!* Mustering all her courage, she turned suddenly and pushed him as hard as she could. He fell back and landed on his butt. Kate cast a quick glance at him as she rushed past. She noticed he was wearing some sort of mask. She was almost to the door and mentally devising the quickest way to unlock it. She knew she then had to open it and get out to the street. It was early. There still had to be people out there.

She was reaching for the door when he tackled her from behind. She went down fast. Her cheek hit the floor so hard, she was seeing stars. Kate didn't have time to recover before he was grabbing her roughly and jerking her up. "Now, why would you run?" he said. He was breathing hard. "I thought you missed me."

He turned her back toward the office. She was dizzy, but she knew if he got her there, she wouldn't have another chance to get away. She wasn't going to make it easy for him. She started thrashing, twisting, yanking, and trying anything to get away. He was strong, though. He put his arms around her tightly. "Kate, you're just making this harder on yourself."

Kate continued to try to twist away, but she couldn't move. He pushed her down to the ground. He turned her on her back and straddled her. He pinned her arms under his legs. She was completely trapped. Then she noticed the knife he had in his hand. Kate didn't move. "Now, that's better," he said, and waved the knife in front of her face.

Kate felt tears come to her eyes. "Why are you doing this to me?" Because of the mask, she couldn't tell anything about his face, but she did notice his eyes. They had no soul. He was looking at her as if she was a laboratory experiment.

"Because, Kate, you're the one." He said this as if he were talking to a child.

"The one for what?" *Maybe if I keep him talking, it will buy me some time. Time to do what, though? Nobody knows I'm here.*

Then she remembered that Mags was waiting for her text. Maybe she would call the police when she didn't receive it. She clung to that shred of hope. She was trying to think of what to do when he took the knife and started cutting off her shirt buttons. Kate started to struggle again. She couldn't let him do this.

"I hope you liked my surprises." He pressed his legs down harder on her arms. She cried out. Her arms were going numb. He continued with the buttons. "Kate, don't you know how special you are? I've been searching for you for a long time."

When he was at the last button, he paused and looked her in the eyes. "I'll take care of you if you notice me." She froze. *What does that mean?* He cut the last button and flicked her shirt open with the knife tip. He didn't say anything at first. He was looking at her chest. "You're perfect."

Kate wanted her whole body to go numb. *Go outside your mind, Kate. Think of something else.* He wouldn't let her, though. He slapped her hard across the face. "Kate, I want you to look at me." Kate turned her face away from him. "Look at me," he said harshly. "Do not make me hurt you."

Kate kept her head still. She felt the knife tip on her chest. Breathing hard, she turned her head to look at him. Kate knew he was going to hurt her. She could see it in his cold soulless eyes. She felt the knife slice down into her chest. Kate screamed in pain.

"Now look what you made me do. This is your fault."

He shifted his weight so he sat higher on her chest. Kate felt as if she were suffocating. She felt the knife slice her again. She closed her eyes tightly and tried not to cry out again. She could feel her blood dripping down her chest and to her arms. *Please, somebody help me!* she screamed in her head. Kate didn't know how many times he cut her, but she felt every slice. She could hear his breathing getting heavier with every cut as if it excited him. She wanted to pass out or die. She didn't care which. She just didn't want to feel the pain anymore.

He was leaning down toward her face. She didn't open her eyes. He was whispering in her ear. "I'm sorry, Kate. I had to do that. You see, I'm not done with you yet. I want other men to know you're marked as mine." He leaned back again, putting pressure on her chest. "Kate, I need you to do me a favor." He said this as if they were two friends having a casual conversation over tea. "And this is very important."

She felt his fingers on her chin. She felt him turning her head toward him. She opened her eyes and looked up at him through her tears. She was trying to concentrate on what he was saying. Her chest felt as if it were on fire.

"Your cop friends. I don't want them anywhere near you." He was looking at her and making sure she was paying attention. "If you don't keep them away, Kate, I'll hurt them. You know I can. Remember the guy in the bar? And Nick?"

Kate flinched. "What did you do to Nick?" she asked in barely a whisper.

He chuckled. "Let's just say Nick won't be bothering you anymore." Kate closed her eyes again. *Poor Nick.* "I'll know, Kate. I'll know if you don't keep your friends away. I know everything that goes on with you. That's me, taking care of you, and soon you'll notice me."

The pressure on her chest left. Kate took a breath. He picked up her arm and started dragging her. This left a blood trail. He was still dragging her when she heard something click onto her wrist. She realized she was being handcuffed to the base heater. He stood and was looking down at her. "Remember my favor, Kate."

He bent down once again and brushed the hair away from her face. "I'll be back."

Then he was gone, and Kate let the darkness take her.

# 8

Paine and Bill were at Kate's apartment. "Where the hell is she?" Paine asked when she didn't answer.

"It's after six. Maybe she had to work late," Bill said.

"Let's go in. Make sure she's not here." Paine started to pick the lock when Bill grabbed his arm.

"What if she is in there, and we walk in on her? She has a gun now. Do you want to get shot?"

"Well, what's your suggestion?" Paine asked through clenched jaws.

"Call her cell phone again. If she doesn't answer, we'll assume she's not here."

Paine pulled out his phone and dialed. "Either way, I'm going in. She can shoot me if she wants. I need to know if she's in there," he said, looking at Bill.

They didn't hear any ringing inside. Kate still didn't answer. "Okay. Let's assume she's not in there. Let's go in," Bill said anxiously.

Paine picked the lock and opened the door slowly. Despite what he had said, he really didn't want to get shot. He peeked around the door. He didn't see Kate. They entered the apartment. *It feels empty,* thought Paine.

"I'll check the bathroom," Paine said as he headed down the hall. He wasn't surprised when the bathroom and Kate's bedroom turned up empty. He went back to the living room. Bill was standing there, looking around. They looked at each other. "Let's go to the bookstore," Paine said.

Paine's bad feeling was getting stronger. They left Kate's apartment. Neither one said anything.

When they arrived at the bookstore, no lights were on. "Maybe she's not here, either," Paine said.

"Only one way to find out," Bill said as they both got out of the car. They walked up to the door and peered inside.

"I don't see anything," Paine said. He reached for the doorknob and felt it turn in his hand.

"Fuck," Bill said from behind him.

They both drew their guns and stepped inside. Cautiously, they started through the store. Everything was quiet. Paine tensed. He could smell the acrid tang of blood. They both saw it at the same time. Paine's heart dropped. *Please don't let us be too late.*

"It looks like somebody was dragged," Bill said in a hushed tone.

Paine motioned with his gun to keep going. Paine saw Kate first. *He chained her to a fucking heater.* "Check the rest of the store," he told Bill, and holstered his gun. He knelt down to Kate and checked for a pulse. Finding one, he let out a breath of relief. He started to check her over. Her shirt had been cut open, and he could see cuts on her chest. *Oh my God, Kate. The son of a bitch cut you.* He gently lifted her head. "Kate, honey, can you hear me?"

"The store's clear," he heard Bill say behind him.

Bill saw Kate for the first time. "Damn, Paine. What did he do to her?"

"Call an ambulance, and then call this in," Paine said through clenched teeth. He took his jacket off to cover Kate. There was so much blood. He saw Kate starting to come around. "Kate?" She started thrashing her arms around and fighting Paine. She gave off little whimpers. Paine's heart twisted. "Kate, honey. It's Paine." Paine was trying to grab her arms to keep her from hurting herself more. "Kate, it's okay. Honey, you're okay," Paine said in a calm, soothing voice. He kept talking to her in a gentle tone. She had stopped fighting him, but now she was crying.

She was looking up at him.

"Have to go," she whispered.

"I know, honey. We'll get you out of here."

Bill came back over after calling the ambulance. "How is she?"

Kate was shaking her head. "Have to go," she said again.

"It's hard to tell through all the blood." Paine said over his shoulder to Bill. "She keeps saying the same thing over and over."

Bill bent down and took Kate's hand. "It's Bill, Kate. You're going to be okay." Bill looked at Paine. "We have to get this guy."

"Don't you think I know that?" Paine said angrily.

"Have to go," Kate said again.

Paine and Bill heard the sirens at the same time. Bill let go of Kate's hand and stood. "I'll go meet them."

"The paramedics are here now, honey." Finally. Paine could hear Bill out front, giving orders.

A few minutes later Paine was stepping aside to make room for the EMTs. He didn't move too far away, though. He stayed with Kate while they treated her and got her ready for transport.

When they were ready to take Kate out to the ambulance, Paine walked over to Bill.

"It was one day. One damn day she was left unprotected," Bill said.

Paine nodded and ran his hand through his hair. "I think our theory is sound."

"I'll call Ben and Jake. Tell them to get their asses over here right away. You head to the hospital with her." Bill looked at Kate. "She's going to need a friendly face when she comes around."

Paine nodded and turned back to Kate. "When you guys are done here, meet me at the hospital," he said to Bill.

Kate tried to open her eyes, but her eyelids were heavy. It felt as if lead weights were holding them down. It would be easier just to keep them closed. She could hear voices whispering. She tried to open her eyes again. She immediately regretted it. The light was too bright. She raised her arm to shield her eyes.

"Kate, try not to move."

*Paine. Why is Paine here?* Then she remembered. She was at the bookstore. The man with the mask had been there. He'd had a knife. She closed her eyes again. She felt tears leak through. She cried harder. She couldn't control it.

"Kate, I'm so sorry." Paine was standing over her and rubbing her arm. Kate heard the guilt in his voice. She opened her eyes and wiped her tears. She looked around and saw four very concerned faces looking back at her. She tried to smile at them, but she was pretty sure her expression fell flat. "Hi, guys," she said.

They all stepped forward. "How you feeling?" Ben asked.

"My chest hurts," she whispered.

"I know, honey," Paine said.

She looked at Paine. He was looking at her as if she were dying. *Am I dying?* "Am I going to be okay?" she asked.

Paine smiled. "You're going to be fine." Then his smile faded. "I'm sorry he hurt you."

"My chest. He cut my chest." She felt tears surface in her eyes again. She couldn't seem to make them stop.

"I know, honey. I'm so sorry," he said bitterly.

Kate reached for his hand. "This isn't your fault." She looked at each of them. "It's not anyone's fault." She lowered her eyes. "He said he wanted to mark me so no other man would want me."

Jake cursed. "That son of a bitch. Kate, we're not letting you out of our sights."

Her heart started beating faster. Her mind was racing. They would never leave her alone now. She could tell them what the stalker had said, but she knew they wouldn't care. She did, though. Kate would not allow these men to be hurt because of her. She really had only one choice. Kate hoped they would understand.

Later Paine questioned her about that night. Could she tell them what the guy looked like? Would she recognize his voice?

"He always whispered. I don't know if I would recognize it." She told him he'd worn a mask. She guessed him to be five eleven. He was thin but strong. She couldn't tell Paine much, but she did tell him what he had said about Nick. Deep down she knew something had happened to Nick. She kept hoping, though, one day he would come walking in with a smile on his face and say, "Here I am."

A couple of days later Kate was able to sit up in her hospital bed. Paine and the other guys never left her alone. At least one of them was always there with her. Today it was Paine. He looked tired and haggard. She couldn't let this go on for much longer. She had a plan. It wasn't a good one, but she didn't see any other way. She took a deep breath and turned to Paine. He was looking at some magazine he had found on a table in the waiting area. "Paine?"

He looked up at her. "Yeah, honey?"

This was going to be harder than she had thought. "I need you to do me a favor."

He threw the magazine to the floor and stood. "Sure. What do you need?"

Kate couldn't look him in the eye. "I need you to get me two things." He stepped closer and looked at her questioningly. "I need you to get me another gun."

At first he didn't say anything. He just looked at her. Kate was afraid she was going to lose her nerve. Kate almost jumped when Paine finally spoke. "Kate, you don't need another gun. We're going to be with you constantly. Where you go, we go."

Kate reached for his hand. "I know, Paine, but I want a smaller gun. One I can keep on me." She put her hand back in her lap. "I know you guys will be with me, but I need it for my piece of mind." She looked up at him. "It would make me feel better having it." Kate didn't like using the pity card, but she needed the gun, and Paine could get it.

He looked back at her with understanding. He laid his hand on hers. "Okay. I'll get you a smaller gun if it'll make you feel safer." He smiled. "You said there were two things you needed, though. What's the other thing?"

*Okay. This is going to be a little harder to explain.* "I want you to buy two disposable phones." Kate peeked up at him. He was scowling at her.

"What the hell, Kate? What do you need disposable phones for?"

She pulled her hand back. "I didn't want to say this in front of the other guys." She hesitated. She wasn't sure how he was going to take this. "I think the guy's a cop." She couldn't look at him. He was probably angry with her for saying it. When he didn't say anything, she looked up at him. He wasn't angry. Kate frowned. *He thinks so too.* She could see it in his eyes. "How long have you suspected?" she asked him.

"Bill and I were talking about the possibility the night you were attacked." He sat back down. "It was just too much of a coincidence that he stopped when we started protecting you. Stalkers don't do that. They're obsessed. They don't just stop."

Kate shivered. She was somebody's obsession. "We didn't hide, but we were out of the way. Still, this guy knew. He knew as soon as we started." He looked at her and frowned. "What makes you think it's a cop?"

She was going to have to be careful how she answered this. She didn't want Paine to know her plan yet. "He said he would know. He would know everything."

Paine nodded and rubbed a hand through his hair. Kate hid her smile. "Okay, but I don't understand the phones. Why do you need them?"

*This is the tricky part.* "I don't trust anybody else, Paine. Just you, Ben, Jake, and Bill." She looked down at her hands in her lap. "I want to get rid of my phone. You keep one of the disposable phones, and I'll have the other. You can't trace a disposable phone, right?" She looked back at him. She saw confusion on his face. She didn't blame him. She thought her story was confusing too. "Cops can trace phones, right?" She didn't wait for an answer. "If he can't trace my phone, he won't always know where I am." She knew it didn't make any sense, and she knew she sounded desperate. She just wanted the damn phones. He was looking at her as if she had lost her mind.

"I'll get the gun and the phones for you," he said after a moment.

Kate tried to hide her surprise. She smiled at him. "Thank you, Paine." He just nodded and looked at her strangely.

Another doctor came in later that day. There been a different doctor every day. This one was a short round man. He didn't look tall enough to reach over the bed. Somehow he managed it, though, and he examined Kate's chest wounds. "They're healing quite nicely, Kate. We have to leave the stitches in for a while, but you should be able to go home either tomorrow or the next day. We'll just have to see how it goes."

"Thank you, Doctor." Kate wanted to ask how bad he thought the scars would be, but she didn't. What did it matter? She couldn't do anything about them. The word *freak* wiggled into her head. She tried to ignore it.

The doctor left, and Paine came back into the room. She saw Jake come in behind him. "Hey, darlin'. How you doing?" He came over and kissed her on the forehead.

"The doctor said I could go home maybe tomorrow or the next day," she said brightly, even though she was terrified. She felt safe in the hospital with Paine, Bill, Jake, and Ben. She wished she could stay there. Kate knew that wasn't an option, though. *I'm stronger than this. I have to be strong. This isn't just about me anymore.*

Paine came over and squeezed her hand. "I'm taking off, Kate. Jake is taking over."

Kate squeezed his hand back. "Don't forget my favor."

Jake was looking back and forth between them.

"I know. I'll take care of it." Then he was gone.

"What favor?" Jake asked.

"Just something I need him to get for me. No big deal."

Jake shrugged and started telling her about his day. They never talked about the case, and Kate didn't have it in her to ask.

The next day Paine brought her what she had asked for. "I'm still not sure about this, Kate." He reached behind him to retrieve the gun from the back of his pants. He had his shirttail hanging over it so no one could see it. He gave the gun to Kate. "It's a P938. It's a concealed carry weapon. Small enough to carry around in the back of your pants like I did."

Kate took the gun and held it in her hand. It was light and easy to handle. "Will this do any damage?" she asked.

"It depends on the type of ammo you use." Paine reached into the bag he was carrying. He pulled out two boxes of ammo. Opening one of the boxes, he reached in and held up a bullet. "This bullet is called a jacketed hollow-point round, or a personal defense round." Kate took the bullet from him and looked at it. She noticed some sort of red plastic filled the point. "When you shoot with that, it expands in fragments upon impact. It hurts, and it will do damage." Opening the other box of ammo, he took out a different bullet and held it up for her to see. "This one is called a full metal jacket." She took the bullet and compared it to the other one. "This bullet could go right through a person. It would still hurt, but it might not stop him or her." He reached for the hollow-point bullet. "I recommend you use this one here. If you're going to shoot somebody, you might as well do it right." He looked at her pointedly.

"I know what you're trying to do," Kate said.

"Oh yeah? What's that?"

Kate sat up straighter. "You're trying to scare me. You don't want me to have the gun."

Paine sighed and sat down. "Honey, that's not it at all. I wish you could have shot him the other night," he said angrily.

"That's why I want another gun. I can keep this one close."

He took her hand. "I get it, honey. I really do. I just want you to feel safe with us." He was almost pleading for her to understand.

She squeezed his hand. "I do feel safe with you. And with the other guys." She let go of his hand. "You guys are the only ones I trust, but I can't let him control me. I can't let the fear win." Tears came to her eyes. "Sometimes it feels as if I might never get my life back, and that scares me the most." Paine didn't say anything. After she wiped at her eyes, she looked at him. "Thank you for this." She held up the gun.

"Kate, you will get your life back. We will get this guy."

She nodded, but both of them wondered when.

# 9

The doctor didn't come back until late into the day. He checked Kate's stitches and told her she could go home in the morning. She thanked him, and he left. Her heart was pounding, and her nerves were on edge. It was time. She looked over at Ben. He had taken over for Paine a couple of hours before. He was sitting in the only chair in the room and playing a game on his phone. She needed him to leave, and she figured she would need at least ten minutes.

Kate cleared her throat. "Ben, could you go to the cafeteria and get me a snack and a soda?"

Ben looked at her strangely. "I'll ask the nurse to get you something." He stood up, came to her bed, and reached for the call button.

Kate laughed. "I could have done that." She punched him playfully. "I just thought it would take too long, and I'm kind of hungry now."

Ben was shaking his head. "Kate, I'm not leaving you here by yourself."

Kate wanted to swear. She had known this wouldn't be easy. "Ben, I'll be fine. It'll take you ten minutes tops. Besides, there are people everywhere." She could see he was considering it. "You could get something for yourself, too."

He shrugged. "I'm not hungry."

Kate let out an exaggerated sigh. "I've had nothing but Jell-O and toast. I need something a little more substantial. I get cranky when I'm hungry, so will you *please* go get me something to eat?" she asked irritably.

"Jeez, Kate. Okay. I'll go." He headed for the door. "Remind me to never let you get hungry." With that parting statement, he was gone.

Not wasting any time, Kate hopped out of bed. She was mindful of her chest. It still hurt when she moved, but it was getting better. She went to the closet and grabbed the clothes she had had Ben bring her from her apartment. She didn't know where the clothes she'd come in with were, but they could burn them for all she cared. She dressed hurriedly, which wasn't easy with her sore chest and stitches. She couldn't put a bra on yet, but luckily, Ben had brought her a heavy fabric shirt. Nobody would notice. She put on her shoes and counted off the minutes in her head. She grabbed the note she had written earlier and put it on the pillow along with one of the disposable phones. She ran to the closet and looked for her bag. She found it and checked to make sure everything was in there. Gun and ammo. Check. Phone. Check.

Figuring she had about three minutes left, she looked around the room one last time. Swallowing hard, she opened the door and peeked out into the hall. She looked both ways and didn't see Ben or any nurses who might try to stop her coming down the hall. Taking a deep breath, she stepped into the hallway. Walking as casually as possible and fighting the impulse to run, she walked toward the elevator. The closer she got to the elevator, the faster her breathing got. She was almost there.

Once she reached the elevator, she pushed the down button. *Come on. Come on.* It felt like an eternity before the elevator arrived and the doors opened. She stepped aside in case Ben happened to be coming out. She waited. When no one stepped out, she jumped in and pressed the garage-level button. She couldn't go out the front door. *He* might be out there. She would go to the garage level and simply walk out. First she had to get there, though. Luckily, the elevator didn't stop at any other floor. When it finally stopped at the garage level, she stepped out and looked around. She was highly alert. She didn't see anyone or sense anything. She saw the exit to the left. She turned and headed that way.

# 10

Greenbluff, Wyoming
Two Years Later

Jack was walking down Main Street in Greenbluff. His long strides were eating up the sidewalk. He had missed the small town he had called home before leaving for Cheyenne. Greenbluff was a small town in Wyoming just south of Billings, Montana. Its population was less than a thousand people, and it really had only one major street. There were two stoplights in the whole town, and he wasn't sure why they needed them. Greenbluff was no Cheyenne, but it was home. He had only left to become a cop, which he did, but after ten years on the force, he had had enough. He didn't miss the life he had left behind in Cheyenne. After his parents had been killed, it had been time for him to come home. He was born and raised there, and his sister needed him. That was five years ago. The ranch was his life now, and he loved it.

The current sheriff kept trying to talk him into joining his staff. The sheriff wanted to retire soon, and he wanted Jack to take over. Jack told him repeatedly he had good people who could take over for him. "Yeah, but they really have no experience," the sheriff always said in his rough gravelly voice. Jack kept turning him down, but the sheriff kept asking. It was almost like a game now to see who would cave first.

Jack was in town to order more grain from the feed store. It was part of his weekly routine. He knew he could have done it over the phone, but it was nice to get away from the ranch sometimes. He loved the work, but he needed a break once in a while. His sister and her husband helped him run the ranch, so he didn't worry about leaving it for very long. Besides, he had another purpose for coming into town. She was about five four with long dark hair. He would love to get his hands on all that hair. Better yet, he would like to see it spread out on his pillow.

*Yeah, right, Jack. You can't even get her to talk to you.* She would just smile at him and ask him politely what she could do for him. This brought up about ten scenarios in his head. *Take it easy, Jack. You're going to get all worked up again.* That was happening to him a lot lately. He would scare her before he even got her to talk to him. He had been at this for several months now. He hoped to wear her down, but every time he would ask her out, she would smile and turn him down. Jack didn't give up easily, though. He was determined to get to know her.

He reached for the door of the Rusty Moose Bar and Grill, opened it, and went in. He stopped and scanned the bar for her. He didn't see her at first, and felt a moment of disappointment. He was like a teenage boy with his first crush. A woman had never affected him like this before. He'd dated his share of women, and he hadn't had to work that hard to get them. He couldn't even get this one to tell him her name, though. He had had to ask Joe, the bar owner. Her name was Kate. He'd tried to get more information out of Joe, but he'd never said a whole lot. Jack always thought that was strange for a bar owner. Joe had told him to ask her. Jack had tried, but she always kept her distance. This made him even more curious about her. He was frustrated, but he never gave up on anything, and he wasn't going to start with her.

He started toward the booth he always sat in when he saw her. She was across the room, near the pool tables. The bar was crowded, as usual. As it was one of only three restaurants in town, it always stayed busy. It was a large open room with tables scattered around and booths lining one of the walls. The pool tables were in the back of the room. A jukebox was in the corner with some country song playing. He'd never been big on country music, which was strange considering where he lived. He preferred any other type of music to country—even rap.

He sat in the booth and waited. He watched Kate interact with the other customers. She didn't seem to have trouble talking with them.

He tried to watch her out of the corner of his eye. She was lovely. She moved with grace and ease. He could sit there all day and just watch her. However, he thought that would probably scare her. He was trying hard to avoid that. She seemed a little skittish. One of the other waitresses was passing by his table. He thought her name was Mandy or Amanda. It was something like that.

"Hey, Jack. How goes it?"

"Um, good."

She was pretty with green eyes and blond hair that came to her chin. She even had a nice body. He probably wouldn't have to work that hard to get her either. She didn't get his blood moving like the mysterious Kate did, though.

He knew the moment she spotted him. Her body tensed, and she stood staring back at him. After a slight hesitation she smiled at him and moved toward the bar. Jack didn't know if it was good or bad that he made her tense. He was going to take it as a good sign. At least she noticed him.

He kept watching her. It was hard not to. She was gorgeous. He noticed he wasn't the only man looking at her. He found himself clenching his fist. *Is this jealousy?* He wasn't usually a jealous man. *Oh, man. You've got it bad.*

He watched her as she approached his table. Her watched the sway of her hips and the way her jeans clung to her legs. She never wore tight shirts like the other girls, but to Jack it made her even sexier.

"What can I get you today?" She smiled.

"Hello, Kate. How are you?"

"I'm fine. Do you know what you want?" She looked around at the other customers. Jack knew she was trying to tell him she was busy and to hurry up, but he didn't care.

"I want you to go out on a date with me," he said, and gave her what he had been told was his sexy smile.

She laughed. "You are—"

"Persistent?" Jack cut in.

"I was going to say annoying."

"Come on, Kate. One date. If you don't want to go out with me again after that, then I'll leave you alone and won't ask again."

She started to say something, when they heard yelling. They turned in the direction of the noise. Four men were drinking and playing pool, and two of them were arguing and getting louder.

"Excuse me," Kate said.

He watched as Kate went back to the bar and said something to the other waitress. Mandy—or Amanda—was shaking her head. She tried to grab her when Kate started moving toward the men.

*She's not going to try to break that up, is she?* Once she'd reached them, she said something to them. Jack couldn't hear what they were saying because of the country song. One of the men grabbed her arm. Fury came over Jack. He started to slide out of the booth, but Kate grabbed the hand holding her arm. She had a death grip on it and was bending back the man's middle finger. The man roared in pain and tried to grab her with his other hand. Before he could touch her, she brought up her right foot and slammed it down on the man's foot. In a quick move she lifted up her knee and hit him in the groin. She was still holding the guy's hand when the man went down. Jack almost felt sorry for the guy, but this was fun. Then he noticed the other three guys starting to crowd her. That was his cue.

*Stupid jerks. All I wanted them to do was keep their voices down. Is that so hard? Then that big ox had to grab my arm.* Kate had just reacted. Now she was in a pickle. The one guy was down, but now she had three others to worry about. She was feeling a little alarmed, when she felt somebody come up behind her.

"Hey, gentlemen. Is there a problem here?"

It was him—the sexy one. She knew his name was Jack. She had had to listen to Amanda say repeatedly how "foxy" Jack was, how nice he was, and how amazing his body was. Kate had to agree, but she would never tell Amanda that. Jack moved to get in front of her.

The guy who had been arguing with the ox stepped forward. "I don't think this is any of your business."

"Sure it is. I don't like men who pick on women."

By this time the whole bar was watching. *This is not a good way to keep a low profile, Kate.* She stepped between the men. She put her hand on Jack's chest and looked back and forth at each of them. "Guys, it's okay. Everything's fine. Just a misunderstanding."

Jack's expression looked as if he were ready to take the guy apart. The men were big, but Jack was bigger. He easily had a couple inches on them. The guy must have seen the same expression Kate had. He decided it wasn't a good day to be torn apart. The man turned toward his other two friends, who were watching him. "Help me get Dave out of here."

They started to reach for the man on the floor, when Jack took a step closer. "Not until you apologize to the lady," he said.

Kate huffed. *Really? Just let it go.* Kate reached for Jack's arm. "That's not necessary."

He wasn't listening. The men were staring at Jack. It looked as if they were trying to decide if they could take him.

"I said, apologize to the lady." Jack's voice was hard.

Kate tensed and waited for the men to attack Jack. To her surprise, the man turned to look at her. "I apologize." He didn't sound sincere, but she'd take it.

"Say it like you mean it."

She should have known that wouldn't be good enough for Jack. *Figures.* Kate watched as the man's face turned a funny shade of red.

"I apologize. We meant no disrespect." His lips barely moved.

Kate held her breath. When Jack nodded, she let it out again. The three men helped their friend up from the floor. They were glaring at Jack when they staggered out of the bar.

When the door had closed behind the men, Jack turned to look at her with a big smile on his face. His dimples were showing. *Damn. He's handsome.* She was still irritated with him, though. "I had it under control," she said angrily.

"Really?" He crossed his arms. Kate tried not to notice the way his muscles rippled under his shirt. "And what were you going to do with the other three?"

Kate just stared at him. Kate knew he had her, and Jack knew he had her. This irritated her even more. Without saying anything, Kate turned and headed for the bar again. She wanted her shift to be over so she could go home. Unfortunately, she had four more hours to go, and she still had to deal with Jack.

She glanced over her shoulder and watched as he returned to his booth. *Come on, Kate. Suck it up. Go say thank you. He helped you today.* She should have been grateful, but instead she was angry with him. There was something about this guy. He made her nervous. It was not nervousness because he was creepy. She just hated the way her body responded to him.

Amanda came up to Kate. "Wow. That was something." She looked over her shoulder at Jack. "Man, I wish his eyes would look in my direction." Amanda turned to look back at Kate. "Sadly, he seems to only have eyes for you." She gave Kate a pouty face.

"Not going to happen, Amanda," Kate said.

Amanda winked. "Then you won't mind if I give it a go." With that parting shot, Amanda went to help a customer who had come up to the bar.

Kate felt the stab of jealousy. *Oh, for goodness' sake, Kate. You don't even know the guy. Even though you would like to.* Kate paused. *Now, where did that thought come from?*

She looked over to Jack's table. He was watching her. Straightening her spine, she walked over to him with her chin held high. She would thank him and move on. When she was in front of his table, he just sat there looking at her, not saying anything. He wasn't going to make it easy on her. *Okay. Maybe I deserve the silent treatment.* She took a deep breath. "I...." She grasped for words. *Jeez, Kate. What's wrong with you?* She tried again. "Thank you for helping me." She smiled sheepishly. "I wasn't sure what I was going to do with the other three. I was just going to wing it." She knew it sounded ridiculous. In actuality, she probably would have run for the hills had they come after her, but she wasn't going to tell him that.

"You're welcome." He was grinning at her. She nodded and started to turn to leave. "But it was impressive what you did to that guy. I enjoyed watching. Where'd you learn your moves?"

Warmth spread through her with his compliment. "Around," she said over her shoulder, and headed back toward the bar.

She was going to get him his food so he could eat and leave. Then she realized she hadn't taken his order. Kate groaned inside. She turned around and went back to his table. "I'm sorry. I just realized I hadn't taken your order."

Jack smiled. "I'll just take the burger, medium rare, and fries." Kate nodded and left without saying anything else. Kate was mentally exhausted. Jack always made her nervous when he came in. On top of that, she'd had to deal with the four bozos playing pool. Now she wanted to go home and take a bath.

When Jack's food was ready, she took it over to his table. She could feel him watching her. He didn't say anything, and this made her even more nervous. She jumped when he spoke. At this rate, she was going to have a heart attack. "Maybe we should start over," he said. "Hi. I'm Jack." He was holding out his hand for her to shake.

Kate hesitated for only a second before putting her hand in his. She felt the electric current zing up her arm. She quickly pulled her hand away. *What was that? Did he feel it too?* She looked at him. He had definitely felt it. She could see it in his eyes.

"It's nice to officially meet you," he said, and smiled at her.

Kate didn't know what to say. She had never felt so much like a fish out of water in her life. She used to date, but she had never had this kind of reaction to anyone. It wasn't as if she could act on it, though. She didn't get close to anyone. "It's nice to meet you too. If you'll excuse me, though, I have other customers." She started to leave but turned back and looked him straight in the eyes. "I really do appreciate what you did for me." She gave him a genuine smile and left before he could say anything else.

*Well, damn,* Jack thought. She was all prickly and angry one minute, and the next she was warm and smiling. He had to admit he hadn't expected her to be angry after the showdown with the men. He was hoping she would have been grateful and thrown herself into his arms with gratitude, but he should have known better. If she was willing to fight four guys without thinking anything of it, then she probably wasn't the falling-into-his-arms type. That just made him want her more. He was going to have to come up with a different strategy. He finished his meal, got up, and laid enough cash on the table to cover his bill and leave a hefty tip. He looked at her one more time and left.

Kate found herself disappointed when Jack didn't say anything else to her before he left. It was just as well. As much as she found him attractive, nothing was going to come of it. She learned a long time ago that this was her life—no close friends and no boyfriends. She still had her boys back home, though. She couldn't bring herself to give them up completely. It was probably selfish, but she needed them. They kept her sane. She called Paine once a week on a disposable phone. Sometimes she would get to talk to all of them. She never called twice on the same phone, and it was never the same day or time. Paine would buy a new disposable phone, give her the number, and then destroy the old phone. She would do the same. Paine once joked they should have bought stock in the disposable phone company.

It had taken a couple months for Ben to get over her leaving. She knew it had hurt him. She had told him it wouldn't have mattered who had been with her that day. She would have left. She eventually told them about the stalker threatening to hurt them if they stayed around her.

"Screw that, Kate. We can take care of ourselves," Jake had said angrily.

She had told him she wasn't willing to take that chance. Every time she talked to Paine, he would ask where she was. She never told him. She trusted him, but it was safer if he and the others didn't know. She wouldn't put it past them to come and try to take her back home.

Paine kept her updated on the case, but there was usually nothing to update her on. She knew they were all frustrated. Bill said they were still working it daily, but Kate knew they had no new leads. So for now this was how it was.

# 11

The first year had been hard. She hadn't returned to her apartment the day she'd vanished. She had only the clothes she'd left the hospital with. She had stopped at the bank to withdraw all her money. It wasn't much, but it had helped her get through the first couple of months.

For a while she moved around a lot. She had never stayed in one town longer than a month or two, and she had found employers willing to pay under the table. This meant she had always worked at run-down diners or dirty bars. She found that people at these places didn't ask a lot of questions, and that was what she needed.

She hadn't finished school. She could probably finish online, but she didn't want to take the chance *he* would find out. She had worked hard and saved money to go to school. She had been so close to finishing before her life came tumbling down. She hadn't given up hope, though, that one day she would finish.

She took self-defense classes, and she tried to get to the shooting range as much as possible. After the second year she started feeling a little safer. She didn't feel the need to move around as much, and she stayed six to seven months before moving on. She still had nightmares but not as frequently. Her scars were a constant reminder of that night. She had had to take the stitches out herself. There were six five-inch cuts running down her chest. Over time the redness left, and now they were a faded white. They were still ugly, though, and this was another reason she wouldn't get close to men. She wouldn't be able to answer the questions she was sure they would have. *He* did leave his mark that night, but he hadn't broken her.

Having no car, she still hadn't learned to drive. So, she had been taking the bus when it had pulled into this old, small, quaint town. She fell in love with it immediately. The main street looked like a town out of an old Western movie. It had boardwalks going down the whole street. Even the storefronts looked as if they could be in a Western. It looked like a tourist town. It had gift shops with Western souvenirs, an ice cream shop, and a doughnut shop. She later found out the town considered that a restaurant. There was a diner and a bar.

She had been extremely pleased when the bar owner had hired her. She hadn't thought she could work in another diner. Joe hadn't asked her any questions and had hired her on the spot.

She could never decide how old Joe was. He could be anywhere from forty to sixty. He had probably been considered handsome when he was younger. Life always seemed to find a way to change people, though. Life could offer some good days and then suddenly harder ones. Kate thought Joe had seen harder days than most. His eyes always looked sad. He paid her in cash, and with her tips she did okay. Joe turned out to be a real teddy bear. He didn't say much, but he always seemed to be looking out for her. When he'd hired her, he'd asked her if she had anywhere to stay. She told him no. He told her firmly but politely that she would stay in the apartment above the bar. He used to live there, but he had needed a break from the bar, so he had moved about a mile outside of town. She had figured he just wanted to get away from the people.

At Christmastime last year he had invited her to his home. She had been honored. She was pretty sure he had never asked anybody out there before. She had tried to ask him about his life, but he'd never answered. She was okay with that. She had her own secrets, and he never asked her about them. One day he told her that when life throws you a curveball, you just have to swing harder.

Kate woke up with the sun shining through her window. It had been a good night—no nightmares. She had to be at work later in the afternoon, but this morning she was going to go out and take some pictures. About a year before, she had picked up a point-and-shoot camera on a whim. She had found taking pictures soothed her, and she had also discovered she was pretty good at it. It made her feel as if she was somehow connected to the rest of the world. She never took pictures of people. She felt it was too much like stalking. She stuck to inanimate objects. When she had saved enough money, she traded her point-and-shoot camera for a Nikon SB-900. It was heavier to carry around, but the picture quality made the weight worth it. Kate couldn't wait to see what she would find today.

Jumping out of bed, she headed for her bathroom. First, she needed coffee. She still really missed her daily mochas from the coffee shop back home. After making the coffee, she headed for the bathroom. The bathroom wasn't large. It was just big enough for a toilet, a pedestal sink, and a combination tub and shower. The rest of the apartment wasn't much bigger. It was one room with two large windows that overlooked the main street below. Some of her own pictures decorated the walls. They always gave her a sense of achievement when she looked at them.

After she got ready, she ate a piece of toast with her coffee. After putting her cup in the sink, she grabbed her camera and gun. She always had her gun on her. She wore clothes that concealed it. They weren't always flattering, but she didn't care. She felt safe. She bounced down the stairs. Once she was at the bottom, she had to decide to go left or right. She looked around. When she didn't see anything that wasn't supposed to be there, she headed left. It was a warm day for this late in September, but she knew winter was coming. She was going to take advantage of the nice weather now.

Sometimes it was really hard not having a car. She couldn't drive it even if she'd had one, but she could learn. She just needed someone to teach her. Sometimes Amanda would give her rides but not often. Mostly, Kate had to stick close to the small town, even though she desperately wanted to explore the mountains that surrounded it. Yellowstone National Park and the Grand Tetons were only a hundred miles away, but without a car they might as well have been a thousand. She could just imagine the pictures she would take there. Sighing, she decided to roam around and see what came up.

She had just rounded the corner of the doughnut shop and was changing a setting on her camera when she ran into a hard body. "Oh.

I'm…" Kate looked up and saw Jack. She felt him grab her arms to steady her. Her heart rate picked up. "Sorry. I wasn't watching where I was going."

"Don't be sorry, babe. You just made my day."

Feeling the pink touch her cheeks, Kate tried to move around him. "Excuse me." He took a step in the same direction as her. She went the other way, and so did he.

"If I had known I was going to be dancing this morning, I would have worn my dancing shoes," Jack said.

Kate looked at him, and he was giving her that sexy smile again. She saw the interest in his eyes. *If only I could act on it. Why can't I?* she suddenly thought. *Just this one time.* She was sure he could distract her for a little while. Unfortunately, she had a feeling she wouldn't be able to forget him, and she knew that soon she would have to leave this small town that she had grown to love. She didn't want to get her heart involved, and somehow she knew she would with him. She wasn't a one-night-stand kind of girl. She looked up at him. He really did have gorgeous eyes. They were a green, so deep, they were almost black. Kate heard him say something. "What?" *Great. Now he probably thinks I'm a space cadet.*

"I asked what you're doing," he said with amusement.

*Damn. Was I staring at him?* "Oh, I'm going to take some pictures of that old wagon over there." She pointed. It was an old stagecoach wagon. She had taken pictures of it before, but she was hoping to get some different angles. She was considering making a collage of it for her wall.

He looked over to where she was pointing. "Are you a professional photographer?"

She snorted in an unladylike way. "Hardly, but I enjoy it."

"Have you been up to the waterfall yet?" he asked.

*Waterfall? In Greenbluff?* She knew there were waterfalls in Yellowstone and the Tetons. "No. I didn't know there was a waterfall around here."

"It's about ten miles up the old highway road. It's pretty spectacular."

Kate's heart sank. She could probably walk it if she felt adventurous one day, but she didn't want to be out there all by herself. She shuddered at the thought. Maybe she could ask Amanda. Kate knew he was waiting for her to say something. "It sounds great, but I don't have a car. Thank you though." She moved to go around him.

"I could take you," she heard him say.

Kate turned back to him. She was tempted. "I don't know you."

His sexy smile was back. "This way you could get to know me."

Kate put a hand on her hip. "Don't you have a job or something?"

He laughed. "I have a ranch. It's about twenty miles up Badger Mountain," he said proudly. She thought the pride made him even more charming.

"Thank you for the offer, but I don't think so." She smiled. She didn't want to be rude. "I really have to go."

She turned and headed for the wagon. Kate couldn't help herself. She turned her head to look back at him. He was still standing there looking at her. He gave her a small wave, turned, and left. Kate was tempted to run after him and say she had changed her mind, but what was the point? She headed for the wagon again.

Jack thought about her the rest of the day. This was going to be harder than he had thought. He hadn't expected to literally run into her. He was sure she had wanted to say yes to the waterfall. He had seen how her eyes had lit up, the interest in them. It had been brief but present. There was something mysterious about her. His cop gut was telling him she was either running from something or someone. He sure hoped it wasn't the law or a husband. The gods wouldn't do that to him. At least he hoped they wouldn't. She didn't seem like a criminal, but at this point he didn't think he would care. If it was the law, he could help her. If it was a husband, he could find a good divorce attorney for her. *Jack, my man, you're a goner. You haven't even been out on a date with her.* He was going to change that, though. He was going to the bar that night to convince her to go out with him. He just hoped he wouldn't sound desperate while doing it.

He was just finishing rubbing down his horse, Chestnut, a mustang with light brown coloring and a white stripe going down her nose. His twin sister, Avery, came into the barn. "I always forget how beautiful she is," Avery said, and stepped up to pet Chestnut.

Jack agreed. The horse was his pride and joy. He had gotten her through an adoption program. Adopters had to meet certain requirements for housing the animals. During the first year of adoption, the government still owned the horse. When the year was up, a vet or a humane official certified that the horse had had proper care. After approval a certificate would be issued, and the horse would become the adopter's property.

When Jack was done grooming Chestnut, he walked her over to her stall and put her in. After shutting the gate, he turned back to his sister. She had the same light brown hair and green eyes as him. Except he was exactly three minutes older than she was. He always teased her by saying it made him wiser. She said it just made him older. Period.

Avery took care of the ranch books. She was a numbers genius. Math gave Jack a headache, so he let her do it. Avery's husband, Shane, helped him take care of the ranch. It was a good solution for all of them. Avery and Shane had their own house on the west side of the ranch. He loved his sister, but he needed his space.

"Do you want to come to the house for dinner tonight?" she asked him.

"Nope. Got plans."

"Really? And what might those plans be? A date?"

She was always trying to set him up with her friends or somebody she'd met at the grocery store. Not once did he take her up on it. He did just fine on his own. Lately, though, he hadn't been out much. "Not yet. But soon."

She was frowning at him. "I don't get it. You have a date or you don't have a date?"

He just shrugged. "I'm working on it." Jack turned toward the exit, when she stepped up to him. They were almost nose to nose.

"Okay. What gives? Who is she?"

Jack sighed heavily. "It's nobody you know." He paused. "And it's complicated." She looked at him blankly and then started laughing. "What the hell is so funny?"

"*Complicated* means she doesn't want to go out with you." Avery tried to control her laughter.

Jack felt himself getting frustrated. "That's not what I said, and why is that so funny?"

She was still snickering. "Because I don't think a girl has ever told you no before."

Jack still didn't see why that was funny. "For your information I haven't even asked her out yet." He thought about it. "Not exactly. I mean, I have, but I'm still working on it." He knew he sounded like a bumbling idiot.

Avery reached up and gave him a hug. Jack scowled at her. "Sorry," she said. "I didn't mean to laugh, but come on, Jack. Has anybody ever said no to you?"

"I'm too handsome and charming for that," he said teasingly. His anger was gone.

"Well, I can't wait to meet this girl. She has me intrigued." Avery left the barn.

"You're not the only one," Jack mumbled.

Jack arrived at the bar later than he'd wanted to. He had gotten a call from the sheriff. Jack hadn't wanted to answer, but he knew ignoring him wouldn't make him go away. He had answered and listened to the sheriff give his spiel again about taking the job.

"Jack, my boy, what the hell have you been up to?" he had asked in his raspy voice.

Jack always thought the sheriff sounded as if he smoked two packs a day, but according to the sheriff, he had never smoked a day in his life. "I'm just going to get dinner. What can I do for you?"

This time the sheriff had used guilt on him. He had talked about how his wife wanted him around more. He had said they were getting older, and she wanted to enjoy life while they still could. Jack had politely told him again he wasn't interested. He had his ranch, and that took up most of his time. The sheriff hadn't accept this answer either. He had told Jack to think about it and that he would touch base with him next week.

Jack entered the bar and automatically sought Kate out. He saw her behind the bar, talking to a customer. Looking to the right, he noticed his booth was taken. Not surprisingly, the place was packed again. He headed to the bar. She looked up when he sat down on one of the barstools. She gave him a smile but kept talking to the customer. He rested his arms on the bar and waited for her. When she finished with her customer, she moved to the end of the bar where an older couple was sitting. When she finished serving drinks to the couple, she headed his way. Her hair was in her standard ponytail for work. It swished back and forth when she walked. It was almost hypnotic. When they had run into each other earlier, her hair had been cascading down her back in small waves. It had taken his breath away. Soon he was going to get to touch that hair. He hoped. Otherwise he was going to be taking a lot of cold showers.

"Hi, Jack," she said shyly.

"Hi, Kate. Good to see you."

"Sorry your booth's taken." She smiled and looked in that direction.

"It's okay. Now I can sit here and talk to you." She was looking down and wiping off the section of bar in front of him. Jack couldn't see anything wrong with it. He put his hand over hers. Startled, she looked at him. "It's okay, Kate. I'm harmless. I just want to have a nice normal conversation with you. I want you to get to know me. I really want to take you to that waterfall sometime."

Gently, she moved her hand out from under his. "You seem like a nice guy. Under different circumstances, I would jump at the chance to go out with you, but my life is not nice or normal."

*Definitely mysterious.* "Why don't you tell me about your life then?" As if she knew she had revealed too much, she went back to wiping the bar. "Kate, I'm not asking for forever. Just one date." *I'll get to forever later.* "Come to the waterfall with me. Not even as a date. Just a friend taking you there for lack of a car." He could see she was wavering. He pressed harder. "It's a great place to take pictures."

Jack held his breath. After a long hesitant pause, she nodded. Jack played it cool, even though he wanted to get off the stool and do a little jig. Instead he smiled. "When is your next day off?"

"Tomorrow, but what about your ranch?"

*She sure is worried about my working habits.* "It's okay. It's one of the perks of being the boss. You can take off whenever you want," he said jokingly. "Should I pick you up at nine?"

"That would be fine. I live above the bar. I hope it's a clear day tomorrow. I'll need the light."

After that she seemed more relaxed around him. He ordered his food and ate while trying not to look at her. It was damn near impossible. He was drawn to her like a moth to light. He took his time eating. She would come over once in a while and check on him. He ordered an apple pie for dessert to extend the time. She seemed surprised, because he had never ordered dessert before. She went to get it and returned without saying a word. He ate his dessert and still tried not to look at her. He took his time eating his pie. He savored every bite and every glance he could get of Kate. When he was finished, he couldn't think of any other reason to stay, so he took out his wallet to pay. He saw her heading his way again. "How was everything?"

"It was great as usual. Thanks." They both looked at each other. "Okay. I'm going. I'll pick you up in the morning. Bring a jacket. It's still fairly warm outside, but it can get chilly up there."

Jack set his money on the bar, gave her one last smile, and left.

He was almost to his truck when he saw the arguing pool players from yesterday leaning against it. *Great. How do they know my truck? They must have been watching me.* He didn't hesitate. He walked right up to the one Kate had hit in the balls. "Can I do something for you?" Jack wasn't going to back down. He had wanted to punch this guy yesterday for putting his hands on Kate. He might be outnumbered, but he could still do some damage before they took him down.

"I think you owe *us* an apology," he said with a sneer.

"I don't think so, buddy. You and your goons here"—he looked at the men behind the man who had spoken—"you were picking on a woman. You need to learn to pick on somebody your own size." Jack could practically hear the man's teeth grinding.

"Well, you seem about the right size. Maybe we should pick on you."

Jack gave a humorless laugh. "There are only four of you. I might be the right size, but you're still outnumbered."

The guy who apologized yesterday came forward. "Are you crazy? You think you can take on all of us?"

Jack wiped the smile off his face. "I think you guys are all talk and no action. You're nothing but a bunch of overgrown bullies."

That did it. The first guy took a swing. Jack almost ducked out of the way, but the guy managed to make contact with the side of his head. In response Jack kicked him in the stomach, and the man bent over in pain.

The second guy came at him. He punched Jack in the nose. Jack swung and hit him in the eye. He was going in for another round when the other two guys grabbed him from behind and held his arms. The man on the ground was standing now, and he punched Jack in the stomach. It knocked the wind out of him. Jack tried to kick him in the balls, but he managed to turn his body so that all Jack hit was upper thigh.

Jack yanked on his arms and managed to get one loose. He spun to take his turn with the men behind him, but before Jack could make his move, one of them hit him in his left eye. *Damn. That hurt.* Somebody tackled him to the ground. He was being held down. He took another punch to the stomach. They were on top of him now.

He was ready to try kicking again when he heard a female voice. "Stop!"

*Kate. Why is she out here? Go back in.* The men looked up in surprise. Then the oddest thing happened. They stepped away from him. They were all looking at Kate.

Jack winced, got up, and turned toward Kate. He froze too. She was standing there holding a gun on the men. She didn't look scared. She was holding the gun with both hands. She looked cool, calm, and collected. Her hands weren't shaking, and she seemed comfortable holding the gun. He smiled. *She is damn sexy.* He walked over to her. "I had it under control."

That made her smile. She looked him up and down. "You okay?"

"I'm good."

"You sure? Because you look a little beat-up."

"I was just getting warmed up."

She shook her head and turned back to the men. They were still standing there, frozen. "Look, we don't want any trouble. Just go home."

The man Kate had kicked in the balls went to take a step toward her. Jack tensed. He was ready to take him again, but Kate raised the gun a little higher and cocked it. That stopped the man but not his mouth. "I see you need your girlfriend to hide behind."

"She's impressive, isn't she? Personally, I wouldn't mess with her."

Jack and the man stared each other down. His buddies were backing away and urging their friend to do the same. They knew when enough was enough. "Come on, Dave. Let's get out of here. It's not worth it."

Dave saw people looking out the windows. Some had ventured outside of the bar to watch. He decided there were too many witnesses. He turned to leave. "I still can't believe you have to hide behind your girlfriend." He sneered.

Jack shrugged. "Do you blame me?"

Without saying anything else, the men left. Jack saw Kate lower the gun and put it back behind her back. *Now, that's interesting. Does she always carry a gun with her?* The excitement was over, and the crowd started heading back into the bar.

"Where'd you get the gun?"

"It's mine."

Jack raised an eyebrow. "You carry a gun?"

"Yes, I do. You have a problem with that?" she asked sharply.

"All the time or just sometimes?" He could see she was getting angry.

"Why? What does it matter?"

He stepped closer to her. "Because I'm wondering why you feel you need to carry a gun at all."

Kate shrugged. "If I were a man, would we be having this conversation?" She was clearly irritated now.

"You know that's not why I'm asking." He was getting irritated himself. "You know self-defense, and you can obviously handle a gun." *Jeez,*

*Jack, calm down. You're going to scare her. It sounds as if you're accusing her of something.* When he had himself under control, he started to reach for her, but he stopped himself. He didn't think she would appreciate it. "What happened to you, Kate?" he asked her softly. He saw her stiffen. She started to turn away, but Jack pulled on her arm to stop her. "I want to help you. Let me help you."

Kate looked up at him. He could see tears glistening in her eyes. "I know you want to help, but there's nothing you can do."

Jack didn't know what to do. He didn't like this feeling. *Why can't she trust me?*

"I need to get back to work," she said.

He resigned himself to the fact she wasn't going to tell him anything, so he let her go. "I'll be by to pick you up in the morning."

She stopped and cleared her throat. "About tomorrow. I don't think it's a good idea."

He walked toward her silently. When they were face-to-face, he reached up and put his hands on each side of her face. She looked so lost. He looked down at her lips. Slowly, he lowered his lips to hers. He felt her stiffen. When she didn't pull back to slug him, he took her mouth deeper. *God, I knew she would taste good.* Her lips were soft and sweet. He stroked his tongue into her mouth. She opened for him. She tasted like mint and fresh air. He felt her body start to relax. She was actually kissing him back. She was shy and timid at first, but soon she became as eager as him. "God, Kate," he said against her lips. "What are you doing to me?" He turned his head and smothered her mouth again. She was pulling on his shirt now as if she couldn't get close enough.

Jack heard a noise coming from the bar. When he remembered where they were, he started to pull away. A small sound of protest came from Kate, but if he didn't stop now, he wasn't going to be able to. He didn't want to scare her more than he already had, and this wasn't the place or time.

Gently, he pulled away. They were both breathing hard. He looked at her. Her lips were red from his kisses. She was beautiful. He put his forehead against hers. "I'll pick you up in the morning, Kate." He kissed her on the forehead and turned. When he reached his truck, he looked back at her. "Thanks for your help. It seems we're good at helping each other."

She was still standing there, looking dazed. As much as she wanted to deny it, he knew she had felt the same thing as him. He smiled, jumped into his truck, and took off.

# 12

Kate woke up early the next day. She hadn't slept well. She had been up thinking about the kiss. She never knew a kiss could be so sexy. It had made her feel wild and possessed. She didn't like thinking it, but she'd enjoyed the feeling. When Jack had stopped the kiss, she had wanted to grab him again and finish what they had started. *What's wrong with me? I'm always in control in relationships.* She didn't have that much experience, though. She had been with only two men. She had thought the sex was nice. It hadn't been mind-blowing, but one kiss with Jack was enough to make her melt and beg for more. She couldn't imagine what the sex would be like.

Kate stopped. *What am I thinking? I'm not going to have sex with Jack. I shouldn't even be going with him today.* She had to admit, though, she was looking forward to seeing him. He was the only man who had ever made her heart race just by looking at him. This was exactly why she should call him and cancel. However, she didn't have his phone number. She didn't even know his last name.

She was going into the woods with somebody she hardly knew. Paine would have a heart attack if he knew. Deep down, she knew she could trust Jack, though. Her instincts were saying he was a good guy, and she wanted to spend time with him.

She would give herself this one day. After that she would have to keep her distance. She didn't think she could stay here much longer anyway. Just the thought of moving again filled her with dread. She liked it here. She was tired of moving around. She wanted to be able to settle somewhere and be a normal person. *Is that too much to ask?*

Kate was starting to feel sorry for herself. To try to stop it, she began to think of other things. She was going to call Paine today. That would pick her spirits up. Maybe she would talk with the rest of the guys too.

Kate quickly got ready. She wanted plenty of time to talk to Paine before Jack arrived. She got her camera bag ready and made sure she had plenty of memory and battery left. She always packed extra in her bag anyway. After grabbing a jacket and her gun, she was ready. Glancing at her watch, she saw it was eight o'clock. She still had an hour.

Taking the disposable phone out of her bag, she dialed Paine. On the second ring, he answered. Just hearing his voice made her happy. "Hi, honey. How are you doing?"

"Hi, Paine. I'm good. How about you and the rest of the guys?" She knew he was at the office already. She could hear his chair squeaking in the background.

"We're doing all right. We miss you though."

Kate felt her throat tighten. "I miss you guys too. Very much."

"Dammit, then come home. We can protect you here. Out there you're all alone. And I've got to tell you, honey, it gives me night-mares." Kate didn't say anything. Paine knew she still had nightmares too. "Kate, I'm sorry. That was callous of me. I don't know what I was thinking."

"You don't have to apologize. I know you're worried, but I'm fine. I've got a good job, and I'm as happy as I can be under the circum-stances." Paine let out a sigh. Before he could say anything else, Kate continued. "So, there's probably nothing to report or you would have called me, right?"

Kate heard the hesitation before he answered. "No. There's noth-ing to report." The last couple of times she had talked to Paine, she had felt as if he were holding something back.

"Are you getting to the shooting range regularly?" Now Kate knew something was up. "Kate?"

She decided to let it go. "I'm here. Yes. I go as much as I can." Because she moved around so much, Kate didn't always have the lux-ury of a shooting range. *The turns my life have taken are amazing. Shooting ranges are a luxury to me now.* Kate shook her head. "How are the guys? Any new girlfriends I should know about?"

Paine laughed. "Jake went out with some girl last week. I'm pretty sure it wasn't for her brains, though."

Kate laughed too. Jake always went for the boobs or the butts. "At least he knows what he likes."

Paine chuckled. "That he does."

"And how are you doing?" Kate asked gently. Paine and his wife had divorced very soon after Kate had left. She knew Paine had taken it hard.

"I'm fine, Kate. You don't have to worry about me."

Kate did worry, though. She wanted all her guys to be happy. "I know, but I can't help it. Sometimes you sound so sad, Paine."

"Anything new with you?" he asked, changing the subject.

She decided to let him off the hook. "I'm going to a waterfall today to take some pictures." Kate knew she had made a mistake as soon as she'd said it. She could hear Paine frowning.

"By yourself?"

Kate laughed. "I do a lot of things by myself, Paine. If I didn't, I'd be locked in my room forever."

"But a waterfall? I don't know where you're at, Kate, but that sounds isolated and dangerous. Don't get careless. You shouldn't put yourself in danger like that."

Kate tried to hide her irritation. *Paine is just worried about you,* she told herself. "I am careful, Paine. I have been careful. I just want to go to a damn waterfall and take some pictures. Is that too much ask? Besides," she blurted out, "I'm not going alone." *Damn it.* Kate winced and waited for Paine to say something.

A hard edge was in his voice when he finally did speak. "Who the hell are you going with, Kate?"

Kate sighed. This was not how she had wanted this conversation to go at all. "His name's Jack."

"His?" He definitely sounded pissed. "Kate, are you crazy? Who is he? I'll check him out for you. What's his last name?"

She resigned herself to telling him everything. "I don't know his last name." She rushed on before he could say anything else. "He's a rancher, and he comes into the bar where I work."

"You don't know his last name?" He paused. "Wait. You work in a bar?"

Kate had to laugh at this. "Yes, Paine. I work in a bar. What's wrong with that?"

He cleared his throat. "Nothing. You just don't seem like a bar kind of girl." Kate didn't know how to respond to that, so she didn't say anything. Paine wasn't done, though. "Kate, you can't go with this guy. You don't know anything about him. Especially in the woods. There's no help in the woods." She felt a tremor go through her at Paine's words. "Find out his last name, and I'll check him out. If he's on the up-and-up, then you can go."

*What am I, twelve?* Kate took a breath. *Remember, he's just concerned.* "Paine, it's going to be okay. I trust him, and you know I don't trust easily. I can't explain what it is, but I feel safe with him."

There was another pause. "Honey, I don't mean to go all fatherly on you, but think about this. You've come this far. You can't stop being careful now."

Kate tensed. "Paine, I appreciate the concern. I really do, but you're going to have to trust me. And I still have my gun."

Paine sighed. "Fine, but I'm going to call you every two hours. And you better damn well answer, Kate. I'm not fucking around on this."

"I'll answer, but you have to stop worrying so much. You're going to get an ulcer at this rate, or have a heart attack."

After that they talked about ordinary things—the weather in Portland and the books they had read. Kate appreciated the normal conversation with Paine. It relaxed her and helped her forget. Looking at her watch, she was surprised at how much time had passed. "Paine, I've got to go. Give the guys a hug for me."

"Remember, Kate. Every two hours."

They hung up after that. Kate was a little nervous now about Jack coming. She didn't know how to act after sharing that kiss last night.

*Should I pretend it didn't happen? Yeah. That sounds good. I can do that. Well, I would if I could stop thinking about it.*

They had agreed to go on this little outing as friends only, but Kate knew that ship had sailed. She was giving herself this one day. *What can it hurt?*

Paine had just hung up with Kate when Ben, Jake, and Bill walked in. Bill saw him put the phone in his pocket. "Was that Kate?" he asked quietly.

"Yep, and you're not going to believe this." He motioned for Ben to shut the office door. He filled them in on Kate's plans. He told them she was going out in the woods with some guy she didn't know and she was working in a bar.

Jake responded first. "Why didn't you stop her?" he asked angrily.

"And how the hell do you propose I do that?" Paine fired back. "Do you know where she is? I sure as hell don't."

Bill spoke next. "Did you tell her?"

He was always so calm. Paine admired that about him. Maybe if he could learn how he did it, he wouldn't have to eat Tums as if they were candy. "No. I didn't tell her. I just didn't know how."

Bill nodded. "I think we need to tell her, though. She has a right to know. What if she reads something in the news? If we don't catch the guy soon, it's going to go national."

"As long as we keep the notes quiet and out of the media's hands, then Kate won't know they had anything to do with her," Ben said to Bill.

"I know I keep asking her to come home, but I'm not sure that's the best solution," Paine said.

"Hell," Jake said, "isn't that what we want? To get her to come back here? Where we can protect her?"

Paine was shaking his head. "She's been safe for two years all on her own. Maybe she is safer away from here. The guy obviously doesn't know where she is, or he wouldn't be leaving his calling card."

"Paine, it's going to kill her when she finds out. That's why she left to begin with. To keep us safe," Bill said softly.

Paine knew Bill was right. It was going to kill her. Women were being murdered just so this guy could get his hands on Kate.

"How do you tell her something like that over the phone?" Paine stood and started pacing. "I can't get her to tell me where she is."

"Maybe tell her she needs to come back for the case. Tell her there was a development," Ben said.

Paine shook his head. "I need to convince her to tell me where she is. I can go alone. It shouldn't draw attention that way. Once I tell her, I will let her make the decision."

He looked at the rest them and waited for their opinions. Paine was the man in charge, but these guys had been through the same things he had. Kate meant as much to them as she did to him, and he valued what they had to say. But nobody said anything as they thought it all through.

"We would need to come up with a very good reason why you've gone," Ben said.

Jake was nodding in agreement. "It has to be something we can back up."

They were all pacing now. It wasn't easy because Paine's office wasn't that big. "Depending how far away she is," Bill said, "you could drive. No air reservations to trace."

"You guys could cover my back until I'm out of town. Make sure I'm not followed." Paine liked the idea. "It's good." He looked around at the men. They were staring back at him and waiting for a decision. "I think that's our best option right now."

Paine sat back down at his desk. "But I don't want to say anything to her until we have a plan in place," he said. They all agreed. "Now we have to convince Kate to tell us where she is."

Paine knew that wasn't going to be easy. He had asked her so many times, he sounded like a broken record. He would just have to convince her this time. It was going to take all of them for this. *We'll gang up on her. I don't like that idea, but what choice do we have?*

# 13

*W*here is she? It's been two years. Two long years. He had underestimated her. He hadn't thought she would take off like that—not without her protection. He watched her cops as much as he could, but he couldn't be in four places at once. He tried getting close to them to see if he could learn any information from them. He would follow them to bars and the gym. He hoped to get even a little piece of information, but they never talked about her. He was sure they had some contact with her. He had even hacked into the ringleader's computer once. He looked at his Internet searches and e-mails, but nothing seemed out of the ordinary.

One day at the gym, the blond cop left his cell phone sitting on the bench when he went to shower. He couldn't believe his luck. He grabbed the phone and went through everything on it—his contacts, phone calls, and e-mail. He wrote down a couple of the incoming and outgoing numbers. He checked them out later, but nothing came of it.

He was sitting in his car late one night, watching the older one's apartment, when he saw her. His heart started pounding in his chest, and his breathing was coming in short gasps. It was Kate. She was back. Then disappointment hit him. As soon as the streetlight hit her hair, he knew it wasn't her. This bitch's hair was an ugly dull brown. It looked like muddy water. Rage overcame him. He started pounding on the steering wheel. He wanted his Kate. She belonged to him. Sweat beaded on his brow. He looked back at the woman walking down the sidewalk. That was when the idea came to him. He smiled. He took a piece of paper and wrote on it. He got out of his car and followed her.

He managed to control his anger and come up with a new plan to get Kate back.

He was twenty feet behind the woman. He didn't know how he could have mistaken her for Kate. She wasn't anything like his Kate. She was short and stubby. She moved with the grace of an elephant. She was disgusting. Just watching her made him sick. He continued following her when she turned to head up the stairs of an old apartment building. She was unlocking the entry door when he caught up with her.

"Excuse me." He smiled. She turned and looked at him with a wary expression. "I was wondering if you could let me in." When she didn't say anything, he pulled out his badge. "It's okay. I'm a cop," he said. "I have a friend who lives in the building." He saw her relax.

"Um, sure. I'm sorry. You scared me." She turned and opened the door. He let her enter first. He looked around. The building smelled of old fried food. The paint was peeling off the walls. It was a real dump.

They passed a set of mailboxes and headed for the elevator at the end of the hall. He let her push the button. They waited without saying anything. The elevator dinged, the doors opened, and they both stepped in. When the doors closed, he made his move. When he lunged for her, he was thinking of Kate. She would know this was her fault.

That had been the first. He waited for Kate to return. He lasted a month before his anger took over again. She didn't come, so he killed again. And again. With every kill he became angrier. The police hadn't released the information about the notes. He thought about doing it himself, but he didn't want to take the chance that they could be linked to him. Kate had to know about the notes. She didn't know he was killing for her. He had to find her. Soon.

Jack arrived at Kate's place at exactly nine. He knocked and waited for her. When she answered, he let out a breath he hadn't known he'd been holding. He half expected her not to be there. He thought she would have bailed on him. "Hi," he said warmly.

She had all her glorious hair down. She wore jeans and a button-down plaid shirt—the same kind she always wore. The jeans were snug. They formed to her body perfectly. The shirt was loose, but instead of hiding her figure, it just added to it. He was pretty sure now the loose shirts were to hide her gun. He would bet a hundred dollars she was packing right now.

"Hi," she said shyly. She wouldn't look him in the eye.

*Uh-oh,* he thought. *We're back to being strangers. Well, I'm not going to let that happen.* He reached for her and brought his mouth down on hers. He heard her gasp of surprise. The feel of her mouth on his was like going home. He felt himself getting hard. He had wanted this to be a quick taste so she didn't forget, but as soon as he'd tasted her, he knew it wasn't going to be enough. He tightened his hold on her and deepened the kiss. He felt her responding.

Too soon he felt her pulling back. Now he groaned in protest. He let her go. *For now.* "You ready?" he said.

He could see she was flustered. She had her hand on her mouth. He smiled. He liked having her off-kilter. It meant she wasn't as immune to him as she wanted him to believe. Shaking her head, she turned to the table where her camera bag was sitting. She grabbed her bag and jacket, and stepped through the door. "You have to stop doing that."

He shut the door. "Doing what?" he asked innocently.

She glared at him. "You know what I'm talking about." She pushed him aside to lock her door. When she was done, she turned back to him. "Quit kissing me."

He smiled back at her. "But, babe, I like kissing you, and you like kissing me."

"It doesn't matter if I like kissing you. Nothing can come of it."

Now he was surprised. He didn't think she would admit it. "We'll see."

Heading down the stairs, he put his hand lightly on the middle of her back. He could feel the handle of the gun. *Yep. She's packing.* He loved touching her. She was all soft and curvy—even with the gun. When they reached the bottom of the stairs, Kate stopped and looked around. It was very brief, but he noticed.

"One of these days, you're going to tell me what you're looking for."

She turned to look at him. "What do you mean?"

He laughed and shook his head. "Never mind. Let's go."

It was a little cooler today, but the sun was shining, and the sky was clear. He knew she was going to get some great shots today, and he was going to enjoy watching her do it.

Jack walked her to the passenger side of the truck. His truck was big, and he'd also had it lifted, so it was hard to get into. He opened the door and helped her up into the seat. Even that little contact gave him a hard-on. Jack groaned. This would be a really long day. He went back around to his side of the truck and hopped in.

Kate watched him the whole way around the truck. His legs were long and muscular. He made those jeans look good. He walked with a purpose and confidence. He was smart, handsome, and charming. *I'm in serious trouble here.* She'd been trying to forget about that first kiss, but then he had kissed her again. She couldn't forget if he kept doing it. The man knew how to kiss. She swore she'd felt her toes curl in her boots. She told herself she would resist him, but instead she found herself leaning into him and wanting more. She would have to be more careful from now on. Trying to pound that thought in her head, she turned to him. "How long does it take to get to the waterfall?"

He turned to look at her. "You're not tired of me already, are you?"

"Uh, no. I'm just excited to see it." She turned pink. *Damn. Can this man read my mind or something?*

He gave her a sly grin. "It'll take about fifteen minutes to reach the parking lot. After that we have to walk for about a mile."

Kate couldn't believe she was going into the woods alone with a man. A year ago she would have laughed at the idea. In her heart, though, she knew she was safe with Jack. Deciding to enjoy the day and forget her frightening life, she relaxed. "Your face doesn't look too bad," she said.

He laughed. "Gee, thanks. What every guy wants to hear."

Kate turned pink again. "I meant after last night. You can barely tell you were in a fight."

"I knew what you meant, babe." He smiled at her. "I just like teasing you."

Deciding to ignore that comment, she looked around his truck. "I like your truck. It's really big." If he hadn't helped her getting in, she didn't think she would have managed. When he had helped her into the truck, Kate felt the heat go through her. She had wanted to turn and jump in his arms. He leered at her playfully. Kate realized what she had said, and she turned a darker shade of red.

He laughed again. "Thanks. I bought it the same time I bought the ranch." He glanced at her and then back at the road. "So you really don't have a car?"

She looked out her window. "Nope. No car." She could feel him looking at her.

"How come? It's got to be hard getting around without one."

Kate turned back to him and shrugged. "It's not that hard. I manage. Besides, I don't know how to drive."

She could see that had thrown him for a loop. He was looking at her as if she had two heads. "How can you not know how to drive?"

"Mostly, I didn't have anybody to teach me. As I got older, I was used to public transportation, so I never learned," she said matter-of-factly. He didn't say anything. "I wanted to learn, but it was never really convenient."

"What about your parents? Didn't your dad want to teach you?"

Kate looked out the front window. "I didn't know my parents. I grew up in the foster system. Are you close to your parents?"

A sad expression came over his face. "My parents were killed in a car accident five years ago."

Kate put her hand on his arm. "I'm sorry. That must have been hard."

"Yeah. That's why I left the police force and came back home."

Kate flinched. "You were a cop?"

He must have heard something in her voice because he looked over at her. "A detective."

*It doesn't mean anything, Kate. He's not* him. When she didn't say anything else, he continued. "Now it's just me and my twin sister. Avery and her husband live on the ranch with me."

"You have a twin sister?" Kate would have loved to have had a sister or a brother—somebody to talk to about school, work, or even Jack.

"Yep, and she's a pistol," he said with fondness. "I'd like you to meet her sometime. She would like you."

Kate ignored this. "Tell me about your ranch."

He gave her a long look before answering. "I have five hundred acres. It's more of a cattle ranch, but I do have some horses. My sister and her husband help me run it."

She envied him. She remembered how she had felt when she'd enrolled in school. She had been proud of what she had accomplished. She sighed. Now she felt as if her life had been put on hold. She couldn't make goals or even dream about what she wanted to do. She was tired of the whole thing. Trying to shake off her mood, she turned her body to face him. "Tell me about this waterfall."

Jack started to answer, when she heard her phone ringing. *Damn, Paine. It hasn't been two hours.* She held up her hand to Jack. "Hold that thought." Reaching into her bag, she dug out her phone and hit the button to answer. "Hi, Paine."

"Good to hear your voice, Kate."

She laughed. "I just talked to you less than an hour ago."

"Yes, but that was before you told me you were going into the woods with a complete stranger."

Turning her head away from Jack, she whispered, "He's not a stranger." She glanced back at Jack. He was watching her. He wasn't even trying to hide that he was listening to her conversation.

"Then what's his damn last name?"

She put her hand over the phone's mouthpiece. "What's your last name?"

"Rivers," he said, but frowned.

She liked it. It fit him. She was thinking of calm lakes and rivers and staring at Jack when she heard Paine yelling in the phone. "Kate! Dammit, answer me!"

She put the phone back up to her ear. Then she remembered she couldn't give Paine Jack's last name. He could trace him back to her. "Sorry, Paine. I can't do that."

She waited for the expected explosion. "Son of a bitch, Kate. You're killing me here."

Kate sighed. "Paine, I'm fine. Don't worry."

"I wish it were that easy."

There was a silence on the phone. Kate didn't know what else to say. "I'm going now. Tell my favorite guys hi for me."

There was another pause. "I hope I'm one of those favorite guys," Paine said teasingly.

Kate was relieved and teased him back. "You know it, Paine. You're the most special of all."

She disconnected the phone while Paine chuckled. She smiled and turned her attention back to Jack. He was scowling. "What's the matter?" she asked.

Jack eyes were looking front and center. "So, who is Paine?" Kate could hear the hard edge in his voice. "A boyfriend?"

She had to laugh at that. "No, he's not my boyfriend. Although, sometimes he thinks he's my father." Jack was still scowling when it dawned on her. "You're jealous," she said.

That seemed to make him scowl more. "You're damn right, I'm jealous. I'm not very good at sharing, Kate."

Now Kate scowled. "One"—she held up her index finger—"Paine's not my boyfriend. Two"—she held up her middle finger—"you're not my boyfriend. And three"—she held up her ring finger—"it's none of your business."

"So, who's Paine? And how many favorite guys are there?" Taking his eyes off the road, he glanced at her.

"He's a friend." She didn't say anything else.

"And?" He looked her way again. She was looking out her window. "Kate?"

She turned back toward him. "What do you want to know, Jack?" She sounded annoyed. "I told you, he's a friend, and that's all I'm going to say. Can we please talk about something else?"

Jack was clenching the steering wheel so tightly, his knuckles were turning white. He knew he needed to tone it down a bit. "You know there's something here. Between us." He looked over at her, but she was looking out the window. "Hell."

He slowed the truck and pulled over to the roadside. After putting it in park, he reached for Kate. She still refused to look at him. He turned her body to face him. He put his fingers on her chin and tilted her head up. "Why are you denying there's something here? I know you feel it." He put his hands on her shoulders. "Kate, I've never had feelings this strong for anyone. Ever." When she finally looked at him, he saw tears. "Kate, what's wrong?" Shaking her head, she tried to move out of his arms, but he didn't let her go. "Do you like me kissing you?" He waited. She gave a slight nod. "Do you agree we have something here?" Again she nodded. "Then why can't we see where this goes? We'll take it nice and slow if that's what you want."

Kate lowered her head. "It doesn't matter what I want. It just can't be," she said with a shaky voice.

He tilted her face up to him again. "I'm sorry, Kate. I can't accept that. Why can't we be together?" he said with frustration.

She wiped the tears from her cheeks and raised her head. "What's my last name?"

Leaning back, he scrubbed a hand over his face. "What does that have to do with anything? Just because I don't know your last name, doesn't change how I feel about you."

Kate reached for his hand and brought it to her lips. Very lightly, she brushed her lips over the top of his hand. "My point is, you don't know *anything* about me."

He squeezed her hand. "Then tell me. I want to know. It doesn't matter what it is. You can trust me, Kate."

Taking her hand out of his, she settled back into the seat. "You're going to have to trust me, Jack. It's better that you don't know." They sat silently for a moment. Wringing her hands in her lap, she said, "I understand if you don't want to go to the waterfall now."

Leaning his head back on the headrest, he turned to look at her. "Kate, I'm not giving up on this, but we'll let it go for now." He reached over and held her hand again. "We are going to the waterfall. You can take some pictures. When you're done, we'll have lunch."

Giving her hand one last squeeze, he started the truck and edged back onto the road. They didn't say anything for the rest of the way. Kate peeked at him. It looked as if he didn't want to talk, and she was okay with that. She went back to looking out the window. She hardly noticed the scenery passing by. Any other time she would have been canvassing potential picture sights, but her heart wasn't in it. She hoped she hadn't spoiled the day.

Kate knew she cared for Jack more than she should. He made her feel safe. What could she do, though? A crazed, demented man was after her and those she cared about. Until he was caught, she couldn't have a relationship with Jack—no matter how badly she wanted it.

Jack signaled to turn into the parking area. It was nestled among large pine trees. As she looked around, she saw picnic benches and a building that housed the restrooms. She grabbed her camera bag from the seat and jumped out of the truck before Jack could help her. She landed harder than expected. His truck really was tall. She took a deep breath. The air felt fresh and clean. She shivered. The trees were blocking the sun and made the air cooler.

She went back to the truck to get her jacket. She was trying to reach it without having to climb back in. She felt him behind her before he said anything. "Here. Let me get that for you."

Kate tried to move out of the way, but Jack had pinned her. Her back was against his chest. Panic crept in. She tried to think of other things, but all she could think about was that ugly, horrible night. He had her pinned against the seat. She couldn't breathe.

Kate started twisting and turning to get loose. When she still felt the pressure on her back, she started fighting. "Let me go!" she yelled.

The pressure left her back. She stumbled away from the truck. She was breathing hard. *Thank God. I can breathe.* She took a few deep breaths. She was going to be okay. *He's not here. This is Jack. Oh my God. Jack. I just went crazy on him.* She looked up at him.

He looked as if he was about to have a panic attack. "Kate, I'm sorry. Did I hurt you?" He started to move toward her.

Kate put up her hand to stop him. "It's okay, Jack. You didn't hurt me." *How am I going to explain this?* "I just don't liked being pinned down."

Jack hadn't moved. "Kate, please tell me what happened."

Kate shook her head and laughed. "It's nothing. I'm fine now. I didn't mean to freak out." He didn't say anything. "Please, Jack, can we just forget it?"

After a slight hesitation he went back to the truck. She watched him open the back door, reach in, and pull out a picnic basket and blanket. He saw her looking at him. "Lunch," he said, and held up the basket.

She gave him a small smile. "I've never had a picnic before."

His cocky grin was back. "Stick with me, babe, and I'll show you all sorts of new things."

Kate's heart skipped a beat. She lowered her eyes. This man made her feel things she shouldn't be feeling—dangerous, reckless things. After not feeling anything for two years, she liked it. He made her want to take the chance and try for a normal relationship. She wanted to forget about the crazy man who wanted her to notice him. Kate shuddered.

"Are you cold?" he asked. He was holding her jacket in his hand.

"No. I'm good."

Jack took a hesitant step toward her. He seemed to think she was going to freak out again. "Kate, I would never hurt you. I want you to be comfortable around me."

Kate closed the gap between them, but she didn't touch him. "Jack, can't we forget about what happened? I was being silly. Let's just have fun today."

He gave her a leering grin. "That sounds good to me."

Kate laughed. "I meant at the waterfall."

"Me too," he said. He was still leering at her. He reached for her hand and pulled her along. "Let's go."

She tried to pull her hand out of his, but he didn't let go. "I just want to hold your hand, Kate," Jack said, waiting for her to decide. Kate didn't protest. It felt good. She smiled and was glad things were back to normal. They started out on a worn dirt path. Pine trees surrounded them, and rock formations were scattered around. Smaller boulders were tucked between large boulders. Kate thought on the way back she might stop and climb a couple.

As they walked she asked more about his ranch and what he did outside of work. He asked her about work and what made her want to take pictures. They were all safe topics.

Soon Kate heard rushing water. She couldn't wait to get her camera out. She wanted to run the rest of the way, but she kept pace with Jack.

As they came around a bend in the path, Kate gasped. There it was. It stood tall like a shepherd watching over a flock. The pounding water cascaded over the rocks. The water spray hit her face. "It's more than two hundred feet tall and drops several times, the largest of which is sixty feet," Jack said.

It was the most amazing thing she had ever seen. She looked at Jack in awe. He looked into her eyes and very slowly lowered his head. She watched him as he came closer. When his lips touched hers, she closed her eyes. The noise of the waterfall went away. All she could think about was Jack. He was kissing her so gently, she wanted to cry. She was halfway in love with him already. Kate jolted. *What am I doing?* She broke the kiss and stepped back. He touched her cheek with the back of his hand. "Kate, I'm not quite sure what I'm going to do about you."

She looked up at him. *My feelings exactly.*

He stepped away from her and smiled. "You ready to take some pictures?"

As she came out of the trance Jack seemed to have put her in, she slung her camera bag from her shoulder. She bent down and pulled her lens from the bag and put it on her camera. She made some adjustments to the camera to get the best exposure. When she was ready, she stood and started taking pictures.

Jack spread the blanket on a flat spot near a clump of trees. He put the picnic basket on top. He sat down and leaned on one elbow. He spread his legs out and watched her work. She moved into different positions and tried to get different angles. Some of those moves gave him pretty good views. *She definitely had the right equipment,* he thought. And he wasn't just talking about the camera. She'd turn the camera different ways too. After every couple of shots she'd look at the screen to view a picture. She usually made some kind of adjustment on her camera then took the same shot again.

She looked happy and relaxed. He liked seeing her this way—her guard down and enjoying life. He knew it wouldn't last long, though. She had secrets she didn't want to share with him. He decided she was running from something, but it wasn't the law. He had to admit, he was relieved about that. He hadn't known what to do for her back at the truck. When she had started fighting him, he knew immediately something was wrong. Somebody had obviously hurt her. His gut clenched at that thought. She had tried to blow it off as if it were nothing, but he was frustrated as hell she wouldn't tell him.

Apparently, though, she had a friend name Paine. What kind of name was Paine, anyway? He felt that tug of jealousy again. She had said he was just a friend. He was certain this guy had something to do with whatever was going on in her life, though. Maybe he could get more information on him. If he could get a last name, maybe the sheriff could check him out. He could do that with Kate, too, but would she give him her real name? *Dammit. I want her to tell me! I want her to trust me.* He could tell she cared about him. He could *feel* it when they kissed. He knew he would wear her down eventually. He just hoped she would be around long enough for him to do it. His gut was telling him he was on a clock with her.

Kate shot pictures for more than an hour. He didn't know anyone could take so many pictures of one subject, but she eventually came over and sat down on the blanket next to him. "That was awesome. I'm sure I got some great shots," she said with excitement. "Thank you for bringing me here."

She made him feel as if he had just swooped up and saved her from a burning building like Superman. He smiled. "You're welcome. I told you it would be worth it."

Kate turned her face up to the sun and enjoyed the warmth on her skin. "It's so nice here."

*God, she's the most beautiful woman I've ever seen.* He could feel his jeans getting tight again. It couldn't be good for him to have a permanent hard-on. He cleared his throat. "Are you hungry?"

She turned back to him and smiled. "I'm starving."

Jack started pulling things out of the picnic basket. "My sister packed this for me. She said it was leftovers from their dinner last night."

Kate started opening containers. The first one she opened had fried chicken in it. She smiled. "I don't think I've ever had real fried chicken before."

That made him stop what he was doing. He gave her a lopsided grin. "Versus fake fried chicken?"

She laughed and slapped his arm. "You know what I mean. The guy with the white beard."

He made a mock horrified face. "You can't ever tell my sister you used the white beard guy when talking about her fried chicken. She takes her fried chicken very seriously."

She laughed and crossed her heart. "I promise. Girl Scout's honor."

Along with the chicken came potato salad and coleslaw. She took a bite of chicken. Her eyes widened. "Oh my gosh. This is really good."

He smiled. "You have nothing to compare it to except the guy with the white beard."

"True." Her eyes twinkled.

They ate the rest of their lunch in silence. When they were almost finished, he reached in the basket again and offered her bottled water. She opened it and took a few swallows. Jack watched as her tongue come out and licked the last drops off her mouth. He reached for her. He couldn't help himself. He needed another taste. To his surprise, she came willingly. He gently guided her down to the blanket so she was on her back, and he was on top of her. She arched in pain. "My gun," she said, and reached underneath her to pull it out.

Jack moved back and smiled. "Well, this is a first for me." She looked at him questioningly. "I have a beautiful woman beneath me whom I want desperately, but I have to wait until she removes her gun."

She smiled back. "A girl can't be too careful."

He noticed she put it where she could still reach it. Jack didn't mind. All he wanted was her. He bent down and laid his mouth over hers. He would never tire of kissing her. His tongue probed inside her mouth. She made a small sound from the back of her throat and opened her lips. This allowed him to move in. It was pure heaven. They met tongue to tongue. He deepened the kiss while his hands started roaming. He reached under her shirt and ran his hand over her flat stomach. He was rock hard. He pressed his hips closer to her thigh. He wanted her to feel what she did to him.

Her own hands started roaming his body. They started on his shoulders and ran down his arms. Next they moved to his chest. He was having trouble breathing. Her hands started inching lower. He brought his hand from under her shirt and reached for her shirt button. He felt her stiffen.

"Don't." She placed her hand over his.

He eased back and looked at her. "What's the matter?" She had her eyes closed. He saw a tear snake down her temple. "Kate, open your eyes." She shook her head. "Kate, honey, it's okay. Just talk to me," he said gently.

She opened her eyes. More tears came. She was looking at him with such sadness. It felt as if it would tear his heart out. "Can you tell me what's wrong?" he asked, and wiped the tears from her face.

She brought his hand to her lips and kissed it. "You are a nice, sweet, beautiful man. You deserve someone nice and normal."

He frowned. "Kate, I don't know what you're talking about. All I want is you."

She pushed him back so she could sit up. "You must think I'm a total basket case. I haven't cried in a long time, but around you, it seems to be all I do."

"Kate, I don't think you're a basket case. I think something happened that has you scared."

She nodded and took a shaky breath. "I can't tell you everything, but you deserve to know some things."

Jack held his breath. He knew she was building up her courage, so he waited. He saw her hands shake when she reached up to put a strand of hair behind her ear. She rested both hands in her lap and looked at him. "I was hurt a while ago." Jack stiffened. *Hurt how?* She looked back down at her hands. "I have scars."

Jack let out a sigh of relief. *Does she really think I would care about a few scars?* He took ahold of her shoulders. "Kate, I don't care about scars. I think you're the most beautiful woman I know. Inside and out."

She looked back up at him. "Jack, you have to know I want you. More than my next breath, but I'm not ready for this. I thought I could do it, but I can't do this to you."

He shook her shoulders gently. "Do what to me, Kate? We both want each other. It's as simple as that. I can wait. I told you we can go slowly." He let go of her shoulders and took her hands in his. "I know you're scared of something." He waited until she met his eyes. "But I think I'm halfway in love with you, and I think you are with me." When she didn't deny it, he went on. "Whatever has you scared, we can deal with it together. When you're ready to tell me, I'll be here." He lifted her chin and kissed her softly on the mouth.

When they broke apart, she rested her forehead against his. "You're pretty sure of yourself," she teased.

He leaned away from her. "Babe, with you I'm not sure of anything." He looked at his watch. "We should probably go." He started picking up the remains of their lunch.

Kate jumped up in panic. "What time is it?"

"Almost one. Why?"

"Oh, crap." She tried to pull her phone out of her pocket. "Oh, crap." After flipping the phone open, she noticed she didn't have any bars. "He's going to shoot me."

"Who's going to shoot you?" Jack asked in a panic. He watched as she lifted her phone into the air and looked for service. "Dammit, Kate. Who's going to shoot you?"

"Paine. He's probably having a heart attack as we speak." She looked back at Jack absently. She reached down for her gun and jacket and started running for the path. She looked over her shoulder at Jack. She saw he wasn't moving, so she ran back to him and started helping put things away. She threw the containers into the basket, not caring how they went in. Jack bent down to pick up the blanket. He was starting to fold it when he saw the back of Kate taking off down the path. "Dammit." *She's going to break something if she doesn't slow down.*

Forgetting about folding the blanket, he grabbed the basket and took off after her. When he finally caught up to her, he was breathing hard. He had thought he was in good shape, but clearly he needed to hit the gym more often. He reached for her arm to slow her down. "Kate, slow down before you fall." *And let me catch my breath.* She slowed her pace to a fast walk. "Kate, we're going to have to have a serious talk about this Paine guy. Because he's becoming one."

She smiled at his joke. "He said that to me once."

They didn't say anything else until they reached his truck. Kate checked her phone again. "Get in, Jack. I still don't have service." She opened the truck door and tried to jump in. She reached for the handle to heave herself inside, but she couldn't grab it. She made several attempts. Jack was laughing. She turned and glared at him. "Could you please help me instead of standing there, laughing at me?"

Still smiling, he went to help her in. Once she was settled, he closed the door and ran around to his side. He started his truck and pulled away. "Finally," he heard Kate say after a few minutes. When he looked at her, she was dialing a number. There was never a dull moment with her. That was for sure.

Kate was not looking forward to this conversation. She waited for Paine to pick up. She didn't have to wait long. "Kate?" he said in relief.

"Hi."

"Hi? That's all you have to say? I've been calling you nonstop for the last hour."

"I'm sorry, Paine. I didn't have cell service."

That didn't seem to appease him. "I called all the guys in. We were getting ready to call in the National Guard. What would be the point, though? We don't know where you are," he said flatly.

Before she could say anything, she heard him passing the phone to someone. "Kate?" It was Ben.

She smiled. "Hi, Ben," she said affectionately.

"Hi, honey. I have to tell you, we all lost about ten years off our lives over here."

Kate sighed. "I'm sorry, Ben. I didn't think about not having service."

"We're just glad you're all right. Keep your pants on, Jake. I'm almost done here." That made her smile. "I'm glad you're okay. Jake's hovering like a mother hen, so I better put him on. You take care of yourself. We'll talk to you soon."

She heard Jake say "jackass." Then he was on the phone. "Hi, darlin'."

"Hey, Jake."

"How's my favorite girl?"

"I'm doing well."

"That's good, because I'd hate to have kick this mystery guy's ass."

Kate laughed. "I appreciate the offer, but it won't be necessary." She turned to look at Jack. *Yep. He's still listening.* He didn't look amused, either. Jake was saying something, so she turned her attention back to him. "Well, duty calls. We miss you, darlin'."

"I miss you guys too. Is Bill there?"

Bill came on the line. "Hi, Kate," he said softly. "It's good to hear your voice."

"Yours too."

"You be damn careful out there. I promise we'll get you home," he said gruffly.

Kate felt the lump in her throat. She was not going to cry. She heard Paine come on the line again. "Okay, honey, I better get back to it. Want to tell me where you're at yet?"

She ignored the question. "Paine, get some rest. You sound tired."

"You take care too."

They hung up. Kate wondered if she would ever get to go home. *Do I want to go home?* She definitely wanted the stalker caught, but would she go back to Portland? She had always thought she was a city girl. She had liked the hustle and bustle of city life, but after living in mostly smaller towns, she wasn't sure if she could go back. Maybe it was just this town. *Admit it. It's mostly because of the man sitting next to you.* She looked over at Jack. She loved just looking at him—the sharp angles of his face and his strong chin. He was right. She was halfway in love with him already. She shouldn't have let it happen, but she hadn't even realized it. Why fight it? She wanted this little piece of happiness. Yes, her life was in chaos, she didn't know how much longer she could stay, and she knew she would have to go eventually.

"What are you thinking about, Kate?"

If nothing else, she could be honest with him. "You," she said.

He turned to look at her. She saw the longing in his eyes. "I like the sound of that."

*I can't give him false hope.* She pressed on before she lost her nerve. "I care for you. More than I should."

She heard him gasp. Before she knew it, he was pulling over to the side of the road again. Once he was parked, he reached for her. "Kate," he said in a husky voice. He kissed her. His kiss was demanding. He wanted more. She put her arms around his neck and gave back as much as he took. It felt right. This was where she should be.

Unfortunately, reality had a way of rearing its ugly head. With every ounce of willpower Kate had, she pushed back from him. "I want you, Jack." She went on before he could say anything. "But that doesn't mean anything has changed."

He reached for her again. "Like hell, it doesn't. I want you too, Kate. I want us to be together."

She put her hand on his chest and shook her head. "I told you before. My life is not normal."

He entwined his fingers with hers. "I don't care about that. As long as we're together, I can deal with whatever it is."

She looked at him. "But don't you see? You shouldn't have to deal with it. It's my problem, and I won't put you in danger." When he tried to speak, Kate put her finger on his lips. "Shh. Listen, Jack. You have to let me finish." She pulled away completely then. She couldn't think straight when he was touching her. "This is going to be hard for you to understand, and I'm sorry. If I stay, I'm putting you in danger, and I'm not willing to let that happen."

He scrubbed a hand over his face. "Can I ask you a question?" She nodded. "Those men you were talking to—they're part of this, aren't they?"

She nodded again. "They were trying to help me." She paused. "They're still trying to help me." She took his hand again. "I wanted you to know my feelings, but I can't make you any promises."

He was looking down at their hands and absently rubbing this thumb across her hand. "I'm not going to pretend I understand what's going on. I don't. But can we make a deal?" He looked up at her then. "When you feel you need to leave, you have to tell me." When she didn't respond, he added, "That's all I'm asking, Kate."

She wondered if she would be able to leave him if she made that promise. She thought she at least owed him that much though. "As long as you promise not to stop me."

He kissed her hand and scooted back over to his seat. "I guess this means I'm your boyfriend." He gave her a wink, started the truck, and pulled onto the road again. Later she realized he hadn't promised her anything.

# 14

For the next couple of weeks, Kate saw Jack as much as possible. He would be waiting for her when she got off work. It was usually late, so they would go to her apartment and talk.

When he had brought her home from the waterfall, he had walked her to her door and kissed her on the cheek. He had never pushed her into anything more than just a few kisses. She appreciated that, but now she wanted more.

She had a feeling she was going to have to make the first move. *Can I do it? Can I take that next step? He'll see my scars. Am I ready for that?* She wanted Jack, so she figured she must be ready. She would be the aggressor. She smiled at his inevitable surprise. She kept telling herself she should leave before it went any further, but every time she thought she was ready to leave, something held her back. Now she was ready to attack him the next time she saw him.

She had the next day off. Jack had told her he wouldn't be able to see her that night but for her to be ready early the next day. He had a surprise for her. She was disappointed they wouldn't see each other that night, but it would give her time to work on her waterfall pictures.

She talked to Paine, and he still seemed to be holding something back. When she asked him about it, he told her he was working on a lead but he didn't want to say anything yet.

"Is it something about the case? What happened?"

He told her something had happened and he would talk to her in the next few days. She tried to press him for more, but he wouldn't budge. Then she got angry.

"Dammit, Paine. This is my life we're talking about. I have a right to know." She immediately regretted her harsh words. She knew this case had become his life as well. "I'm sorry, Paine. I just want this to be over."

He sighed. "I know you do, honey, and so do I. But I have to work some things out first, and then we'll talk. Okay?"

Now she was anxious. It was probably a good thing she wouldn't see Jack tonight. He would know something was wrong. She found herself wanting to tell him everything so many times. She kept telling herself he had a right to know. However, it still came down to her having to leave, so she never told him.

She was taking a tray of empty glasses back to the bar when somebody grabbed her arm. Her first instinct was to jerk her arm away, but she had dealt with this guy before. She sighed and turned. She thought maybe she should have taken the diner job. "Yes, sir? What can I do for you?" This guy had been a problem before. He'd been in a couple of times and always drank too much. He wasn't dangerous—just bothersome. Tonight wasn't any different.

He was smirking. "Well, sweetheart, to start, you can do me."

Kate rolled her eyes. She tried wrenching her arm loose, but he squeezed harder. *Okay. A little too hard.*

She looked him in the eye and then at his hand holding her arm. "I'll give you five seconds to let go of my arm," Kate said in a menacing voice.

The man stood up too quickly, and then chaos broke out. The man was too drunk. He tried to grab on to something so he wouldn't fall. He still had ahold of Kate's arm, and they both fell. He landed on top of her. Her head slammed to the floor, and his head smacked her hard in the eye. Her tray went flying, and broken glass went everywhere.

She was lying on the floor, trying to catch the breath that had been knocked out of her. She could hear Amanda yelling. Amanda was trying to get the drunk guy off her, but she couldn't do it alone. The drunk man was also trying to get up and was using Kate for leverage. The pressure would ease, Amanda would lose her grip, and down the man would go again. After the third try, Kate told Amanda to stop.

Amanda was looking wide-eyed down at Kate. "I'm sorry, Kate. What should I do? I think he just passed out."

If the person in the situation hadn't been her, Kate probably would have thought the whole thing was funny. Kate squeezed her arm out from under the man. Once she had, she pushed and rolled him at the same time. The man flopped onto his back. Kate still didn't get up. *Just a few more gulps of air.* Amanda was still looking at her with concern.

"It's okay, Amanda. Just catching my breath." Her head and eye hurt. Her ribs didn't feel that great either.

Once she had her breathing under control, she sat up. *A little dizzy but not bad. You're almost there, Kate,* she kept telling herself. She put her hand down to help herself up, when she felt the glass cut into her palm. She quickly brought her hand to her chest. She looked down and saw the blood first. Then she saw the piece of glass sticking out of her hand. *Damn. This just isn't my night.*

"I think I'm going to be sick." Amanda was almost gagging.

Two men reached down to help Kate up. *Where were they five minutes ago?*

"You okay, miss?"

*Just peachy.* "I'm fine. Thank you." Amanda was bouncing from one leg to another and wringing her hands. "Amanda, could you get me a towel please?"

"Right."

Amanda left and came back with the towel. Kate took the towel and put it under her hand. She was bleeding all over the floor. "If you start cleaning up the glass, I'll take care of this and come back to help you."

Amanda nodded and started picking up glass. Kate went to the back room and grabbed the first aid kit. Then she headed for the women's restroom.

She turned on the tap and put her hand under the cold running water. She hissed when it hit her hand, but she needed to clean off the blood to see how deep the glass was in. Once the blood was gone, she decided it wasn't bad. She started pulling the glass out. *It hurts like hell,* she thought. She finally worked all of it loose. The blood was coming faster now. She left her hand under the water until the flowing blood lessened. She dried her hand with a clean towel and put an antibacterial ointment on it. She took some gauze and wrapped her hand several times. Figuring that was the best she could do with one hand, she started cleaning up her mess. She looked down at her shirt and saw she had blood all over it. She was going to have to change. *And take some aspirin. My head is killing me.*

When she returned to the front of the bar, she noticed the drunk was gone. Amanda was still cleaning up, so Kate bent down to start helping. "Where'd the guy go?" she asked.

Amanda looked at her and then at her shirt. "Those two men dug the keys out of the guy's pants and took him outside to put him in his car. He'll sleep it off there." Amanda stood. "Kate, your shirt's a mess."

Kate stood too. "I know. I'm going to have to change."

"Your eye doesn't look so good either," Amanda said. She looked at Kate's face and then around at the bar. "Listen, you go home. I've got this." Kate started to protest, but Amanda cut her off. "It's almost closing time anyway. There are only a few customers. And no offense, but you look like you've been beaten up."

Kate wanted to go. Her whole body hurt—her head, her ribs, and her hand, especially. She wanted to go to her bed and collapse. She looked around and saw only a few customers left. "Okay. If you're sure."

Amanda started pushing her toward the door. "Go. Have a good day off tomorrow."

Kate left and started up the stairs to her apartment. She grabbed the railing and slowly worked her way up. Her whole body was protesting. She had never realized before how many stairs there were.

She made it to her door, unlocked it, and went in. Too tired to do anything else, Kate pulled her bloody shirt over her head and threw it onto the floor, grabbed a T-shirt out of the dresser, and fell into her bed. Her last thought before sleep took her was that she had to be up early. Jack was coming.

Jack was knocking at Kate's door. When she didn't answer, he knocked again. *Where the hell is she?* Growing concerned, he pounded on the door. "Kate?" He finally heard some movement inside. He let out a relieved breath and waited. He heard the door being unlocked, and it swung open.

"Come in, Jack," Kate said. She turned away and headed for the bathroom. "I'm sorry. I must have overslept."

Jack heard the bathroom door close. He came in and shut the front door. The first thing he noticed was the bloody shirt on the floor. He reached down and picked it up. *What the hell?* He rushed over to the bathroom. He knocked. "Kate? Babe? Are you hurt? I saw your shirt on the…"

The bathroom door opened, and he saw her face. "My God, Kate. What happened to you?" He reached for her.

She waved him off. "It's not a big deal. There was an accident at work last night."

She tried to move around him, but he took her arm and spun her around to face him. "Not a big deal? Have you seen your eye? A prizefighter would be proud." Then he saw her bandaged hand. "And what happened there?" His voice was getting louder. She looked as if she had been in a fight. He stiffened. "Did somebody hurt you?" He saw her wince. "You're in pain. What's hurting you?"

She pulled away again and sat on her bed. "Jack, you have to lower your voice. My head is killing me." She put her fingers on her temples and started to rub them.

Jack sat down next to her. "I'm sorry, Kate. Why does your head hurt?" *How badly is she injured? Should I take her to the hospital?* He was trying to stay calm, but he couldn't stand to see her hurting. He put his arm around her and hugged her. She yelped in pain. Jack immediately pulled away. "What did I hurt?"

She reached for his hand. "It's okay, Jack. It's my ribs."

Very gently, he turned her so she was facing him. "Who hurt you?" he said in a steely voice.

Kate shook her head. "It was all an accident." She told him about the drunk and cutting her hand on the broken glass. "If you think about it, it was actually kind of funny."

He wasn't amused. "Why didn't you call me?"

Kate shrugged. "Because I'm fine."

He scowled and reached for her hurt hand. "Let me look at this." She held it out to him, and he started to unwrap the gauze. When he got to the last layer, it stuck to her hand. Kate flinched and tried to pull her hand back. "I'm sorry, babe. But we need to get this bandage off and clean the wound again."

Little by little, he worked the bandage loose. When it was free, he brought her hand closer to look. The inch-long cut along the joint of her thumb and palm was puckered and swollen. He didn't think the cut was too deep, though. "I don't think you need stitches. Where's your first aid kit?"

She blinked at him. "Um, I don't have one."

"Why not?" He frowned. "Never mind. It doesn't matter right now." He walked into her kitchen and looked for a dish towel. When he found one, he returned to the bed. "Okay. I'm going to wrap your hand in this towel, and I'll bandage it when we get to the ranch."

She looked at him and smiled. "We're going to your ranch?"

Concentrating on her hand, he nodded absently. When he finished wrapping it, he looked up and saw her face. He leaned in and kissed her, trying not to hurt her. He tasted cinnamon. She smelled like peaches. He pulled back. "Good morning." he said.

She reached for him with her unhurt hand and brought his head down for another kiss. She kissed him softly at first, but soon the kiss turned heated and urgent. It was as if she thought he was going to leave. *Maybe* she *is going to leave.* He pushed the thought away. He wanted her more than anything. He started to push her back onto the bed, but she cried out in pain. "Damn, babe. I'm sorry."

He helped her sit back up, and they looked at each other. They were both breathing hard. He brought his hand up to brush a strand of hair behind her ear. "Have I ever told you I love your hair?" Kate shook her head. "Well, I do. It feels like silk." He ran his hand through it. He leaned in for one more kiss. Very softly, he brushed his lips over hers. He didn't know if he would ever get enough of her. She shifted to get closer and groaned in pain. He sat back. "Are you up for going to the ranch? If not, we can stay here. I have no problem just holding you all day in this bed." He grinned.

She grabbed his hand, pulled him up, and winced. "Are you kidding? I can't wait to see your ranch. Is that your surprise?"

He laughed and kissed her hand. "It's one of them."

She slid her arm around his waist. "This sounds mysterious."

He loved that she was becoming comfortable with him. She was touching him and even kissing him first. He was trying to go slow and let her set the pace. He knew she was almost ready. He was ready, but he would wait forever if that was what it took. He put his arm around her waist and headed for the door. "Do you want to take something for your head?"

She let go of him. "I already did in the bathroom." She turned back into the room. He watched her pick up her gun from her nightstand, check the clip, reach around, and put it behind her back in her jeans. *Damn. She sure knew how to handle that thing.*

She turned and smiled. "Ready," she said with excitement.

It made him smile. "I can't wait for you to meet my sister." He opened the door and turned to wait for her.

She stopped and was looking at him in horror. "I can't meet your sister now. Look at me. I look as if I've been in a bar fight."

He walked back over to her and smiled. He put his arm around her waist and started pushing her toward the door. "Trust me. She'll love you."

Kate wasn't sure about this. *Meeting his sister?* She wanted to meet her but not when she looked as if somebody had used her face as a punching bag.

They left town and were on the highway. It was the same highway they took to go to the waterfall, but they turned in the opposite direction. They passed several meadows filled with tall grass. Wyoming had a lot of wide open spaces. There were lots of room for animals to roam, and she saw deer grazing. They never seemed to be afraid of people. Being a city girl, she commented about how strange that was. Jack turned to look at her. "They get used to people, but you couldn't get close enough to pet one."

Soon they were turning off the highway and onto a paved road. They had traveled about a half mile when they came to a black metal gate with a wooden fence. Kate looked in both directions and didn't see an end to the fence. He had said he had five hundred acres. She just realized how big that was.

Jack pushed a button on the remote sitting on his visor. The gate opened, and they went under a wooden arch with a sign on top. TWIN RIVERS RANCH was spelled out in black metal. She smiled. "I like the name."

He smiled back at her. "It's just as much hers as mine."

Jack pushed a button, and the gate closed. They started down the paved road. Grassy meadows were on both sides. Kate could see a cluster of pine trees ahead. They had traveled about a mile through those trees, when they came upon a clearing. Kate gasped. A sizable log house sat in the middle of it. It was one level with a green metal roof. It had a wraparound porch with four wooden rocking chairs just waiting for someone to use. She turned to him. "Jack, it's beautiful," she whispered.

She'd never seen anything like it. It was simple yet elegant. A barn sat about two hundred feet from to it. Next to the barn was a wooden fenced corral with a couple of horses grazing in it. She had never ridden a horse before. The idea made her a little nervous, but she would love to try. *Maybe that's one of my surprises.*

Jack parked in front of the house. He turned to say something to her, but Kate, bursting with excitement, had already jumped out of the truck. Her ribs screamed at her. She bent over in pain.

Jack came running around the truck. "Dammit, babe. You have to wait for me." She had to take a couple of breaths to work through the pain. He put his arm over her back and bent down with her. "You okay?"

Kate heard a door opening and then running feet. She straightened. She looked over Jack's shoulder and saw a pretty brunette rushing toward them. *This must be his sister.*

"Jack," the woman said. "What's wrong?" She had the same color eyes as Jack. They even had the same nose and chin. She looked at Kate and then grinned. "What does the other guy look like?"

Kate laughed and ignored the pain in her ribs. "Let's just say he had to be carried to his car." They all laughed.

Jack turned to Kate. "Meet Avery, my sister."

Kate stuck out her good hand. "Nice to meet you."

Before Jack could stop his sister, she reached for Kate and hugged her. Kate tried to hold back the groan, but she must have made some kind of noise. Avery jumped back from her. "Oh, Kate, I'm sorry." She turned to her brother and slapped him on the arm. "Why didn't you tell me she had sore ribs?" she asked sternly.

"Because, little sis, I just found out this morning." He looked at Kate accusingly then back to Avery. "And you didn't give me time to tell you."

Avery pushed Jack out of the way and took Kate's arm. "Come on, honey. Let's go inside." Jack walked on the other side of Kate.

"I love your hair, Kate," Avery told her. "I could never get my hair that long."

"Avery, I need to bandage Kate's hand."

Avery looked down. "Oh my. I can't wait to hear this story."

When they reached the front door, Jack opened it and went in first. He disappeared down the hallway. Kate got her first look inside. It was just as beautiful as the outside. The living room and kitchen were one open room with large beams running across the ceiling. The kitchen was all stainless steel and granite. In the living room two leather couches faced each other. Two cream-colored chairs sat side by side with a table between them. An area rug was on the floor in the center of the room. It was very masculine but tastefully done. It reminded her of Jack. She liked it immediately.

Avery led her to one of the couches, and they both sat down. "Let me take this towel off," Avery said, and reached for Kate's hand.

Kate tried to hold her hand back. "It's okay. I can do it."

"Don't be silly. It'll be easier with two good hands."

Avery waited for Kate to make the decision. Kate relented and extended her hand. Avery was just finishing taking the towel off when Jack walked back in with bandages and ointment. He sat down on the other side of Kate. Avery was still looking at Kate's hand. "I have to hear this story."

Kate laughed. "It's really not that exciting."

Avery snorted. "I doubt that."

Jack took Kate's hand from Avery. He started working on it while Kate told Avery the story. When she was done, Avery was laughing. Kate turned to Jack and smiled. "See? I told you it was funny."

"Well, I don't think it's funny," Jack said, and glared at his sister.

Kate glanced back to Avery. She was trying to keep a straight face. Then she and Avery burst out laughing at the same time. "Don't make me laugh," Kate said. She put her hand on her ribs. "It hurts."

"Well, I'm glad you two are having a good time." Jack was more annoyed, and this made them laugh even harder.

But when Kate looked back to Jack, a small grin had appeared on his face, and soon he was laughing with them. A few minutes later Jack announced he was done. He brought Kate's hand to his lips and kissed it. They looked at each other. They were unaware Avery was watching them with a smile on her face. Avery cleared her throat to get their attention. "What are your plans for the day?"

Jack kissed Kate's hand one more time and gently set it on her lap. "I'm going to teach Kate how to drive," Jack announced. Kate looked at him with a huge grin on her face.

"Wait. You don't know how to drive?" Avery asked incredulously.

Kate turned to look at Avery. *There's that "two heads" look again. Maybe it is a big deal that I don't know how to drive.* "Um, I just never learned." Kate didn't know what else to say. Avery started sputtering.

"Wow, Avery. Never thought I'd see the day when you were at a loss for words," Jack said. He grinned, stood, and carefully pulled Kate up with him.

Leaving Avery speechless on the couch, Jack and Kate headed for the door. "If it's okay, I'll show you around later. I want to take you driving first. I'm worried about the weather. They're expecting a storm later."

Once outside, they headed for Jack's truck. Kate was going to drive. *Well,* she thought, *this should be interesting.* She started heading for the passenger side of the truck, but Jack tugged on her arm. "Nope. You're coming this way."

She was digging her feet into the ground and trying to stop. "You want me to drive *now?*"

Jack laughed. "No, babe. I love you, but I'm not crazy." Kate reeled from the "I love you." Jack had his door open and was waiting to help her in. *Relax, Kate. It's just an expression.* "I'm going to help you in. Then I want you to scoot to the middle of the seat. I'm going to drive us to a nice open field where there's nothing in the way."

Once they were both settled in, Jack started the truck and headed out the way they had come in. When they were in the tree section, Jack made a left onto some kind of road. She guessed she could call it that. It was more of a path.

They bounced along, and Kate tried to protect her ribs.

"Are you okay?" Paine asked concerned.

"I'm fine, Jack."

Another clearing came into view. It was a large open field with the same kind of fencing as the corral by the house. Jack drove up to a gate. He jumped out, opened it, and got back in. Once through, he drove to the middle of field.

"What do you use this field for? Why the fence?" she asked.

"We use it for the cattle. We put them in here before we take them to auction. It's easier."

Kate nodded as if she understood. *I'll ask Avery later.*

Jack turned off the truck and turned to her. "Tell me what you know about driving."

Kate looked at him, confused. "I know this is a big-ass truck." She pointed. "And this is a steering wheel."

Jack looked at her. Kate looked back at him silently. Jack laughed. "Okay. We'll start with the basics."

He started telling her about the gas, brakes, and different gears. *Wow,* she thought. *He really is starting with the basics.* She interrupted him. "Jack, I know what all that is. I just don't know how to *drive.*"

"Okay, babe. Then let's switch places." Jack gently lifted her up so he could move behind her. She ended up sitting on his lap. She was trying to get her legs over his, but her sore ribs made it difficult. She realized Jack wasn't moving. She looked back at him. She felt something pressing into her bottom. She felt his whole body stiffen. Literally. She loved the feeling of power it gave her, and she couldn't help from teasing him. She wiggled again. He grabbed her hips. "Babe, if you want to go this round, I'm more than happy to oblige," he said huskily. He knew exactly what she was doing. She quickly scooted over to the driver's seat. He laughed. "Chicken."

Once she was settled, he told her to put her seat belt on. *Really? We're in a field, for Pete's sake.* But she did it without saying anything.

"Okay," Jack said. "Now you need to adjust your seat so you're comfortable while driving." He showed her where the buttons were to do that. Once she finished, she started for the key. "Not yet, Kate." She looked at him a little impatiently. "You need to adjust your mirrors. Start with the side mirrors. Adjust them so you can see what's on each side of you." She looked at him when she was done. "Okay. Now the rearview mirror. You want to adjust it so you can see what's behind you."

"Okay," she said when she was done.

"Now put your right foot on the brake pedal." He watched her. "You use your right foot only for the brake and gas." She nodded. "Okay, Kate. Turn the key."

Filled with excitement and a little anxiety, she turned the key. The engine revved to life. Kate could feel the rumbling of the engine beneath her legs. She turned to Jack and smiled. She liked it.

"Okay. Leave your foot on the brake and put the gear in drive." She reached for the gear handle and pushed it down to drive. "Now take your foot off the brake and just rest it on the gas pedal for now."

She blew out a breath. *Here goes nothing.* She took her foot off the brake, and the truck started moving forward. She yelped. *Is it supposed to do that?*

Jack laughed. "It's okay, Kate. There's nothing in front of you. Now very gently press down the gas pedal." She pressed the gas, and the truck roared. They jerked. She immediately took her foot off the gas. She looked over at Jack. He was smiling. "Try again. Keep your foot pressed to the pedal." She tried again, and they jerked forward and then backward. She eased off the gas but immediately pressed it again.

And yet again, they jerked back and forth. After a few minutes of neck jostling, she got the hang of it.

She turned to Jack and smiled. "Look. I'm driving."

He put his hand on her thigh and smiled too. "Yes, you are. And you're doing great."

She turned back to look out the window. "Um, Jack?" She was frowning. When he didn't say anything, Kate gave a quick glance at him. He was watching her. She turned to look out the front window again. "Jack?" she said louder.

He must have heard the alarm in her voice because he finally turned to look. "Kate, brakes!" he yelled.

Kate was flustered now. She hit the gas pedal instead. The truck rumbled and sprinted ahead.

Jack was putting his leg over hers and trying to reach the brakes. Kate screamed. Jack slammed his foot on the brake. They flew forward and then backward when they ran into the fence.

The silence was deafening. She looked over at Jack. She swore he was green. She looked out the front window and saw the fence. A couple of poles leaned so far sideways, they almost touched the ground. Broken boards and debris were scattered everywhere, and that included the truck's hood.

Seeing what she had done, she was mortified. Kate put her face in her hands. "Jack, I'm so sorry." She had wrecked his truck. He was so proud of it. She couldn't look at him.

She felt her hands being pulled away from her face.

"Kate, look at me." She turned to look at him. "It's all right." He put her hand to his lips and kissed it. "It was my fault. I was distracted." He kissed the other hand. "You looked so beautiful, I couldn't take my eyes off you."

She shook her head and looked out the window again. "Look what I did to your truck." She groaned. "And your fence."

He put his fingers on her chin and turned her face toward him. He was grinning. "If you think about it, it's kind of funny."

She gave him a wan smile. The man was crazy. She had wrecked his beautiful truck, and he was trying to make *her* feel better. If she didn't love him before, she was pretty sure her heart just flipped the switch.

She leaned toward him and pressed her lips to his. He was the sexiest man she had ever laid eyes on. He was kind and gentle. She knew she didn't want to be anywhere else except right here. No matter what it took, she would try to stay. She pulled back to look at him. "I love you," she whispered. Her heart hammered.

He rested his forehead on hers. "Thank God." He let out a breath. "I love you too, Kate. You're it for me. I want no one else."

She threw her arms around him and hugged him. She didn't care about her sore ribs. She knew she was going to have to tell him. He needed to know. *If he knows what he's getting himself into, will he change his mind?*

"Babe, as much as I want to keep holding you, I have to look at the truck." He pulled her arms down, and Kate moved away. He gave her a quick kiss on the lips and moved to get out of the truck. When he opened the door, he turned back to her. "Stay there. I'll come around and help you out." He jumped down and ran around the back of the truck.

He opened her door, and Kate took off her seat belt. *Guess it was a good thing I had it on.* Jack reached up and helped her down. He took her hand and started to the front of the truck. When Kate saw the damage, she groaned again. The driver's-side headlight was broken, and the fender below it was dented. She promised herself she would pay for the damage no matter how long it took her to earn the money.

Jack grabbed the board off the hood and threw it aside. He started pulling the poles away from the truck and laying them along a part of the still-intact fence. He did the same with the boards. Soon there was a big gaping hole in the fence. Turning to her and smiling, he asked, "You ready?" She nodded and headed for the passenger side of the truck. "Where are you going?"

She turned and looked back at him. He was holding the driver's door open. *He doesn't seriously think I'm going to get back in there and drive. No way in hell.* She started shaking her head. "You're joking, right?"

He grabbed her hand. "You know what they say. If you fall off the horse, get right back on."

She tugged her hand out of his and backed away. "This isn't a horse."

He reached for her again. "Kate, you can do this. I have faith in you." He pushed her back toward the truck door, opened it, and helped her in. He ran around to the other side.

Kate's heart was in her stomach. *The problem is, this truck is too damn big. Maybe I should have started with something smaller.*

Jack was sitting next to her. "Okay. We're going to try this again." Kate sat stiffly and didn't look at him. He laughed. "Kate, you look as if you're about to jump out of a plane without a parachute." She nodded. "Start the truck," he said, and chuckled.

She didn't move. Jack waited. *I can do this. I have to do this. For Jack. He's been so patient. He wants me to learn, and I really want to learn too.*

Taking a deep breath, she put her foot on the brake and turned the key. "Good girl," Jack said. "Now we're going to back up, so put the gear in reverse. Remember to leave your foot on the brake." Kate put the truck in reverse and looked at him. "Going backward is no different than going forward." *Easy for him to say,* she thought. "Turn your head and look behind you." She turned her head so she was looking out the rear window. "Now put your foot on the gas, and give it a little pressure."

Kate did, and the truck started backing up. *Well, that wasn't so bad.*

"Keep going until you have enough room in front of you to turn around." They kept moving backward. She put her foot back on the brake. She faced forward again and put the gear in drive. "Turn the wheel to your left, and let's turn around." Once she had the car turned, she stopped again. "Whatcha waiting on, babe? Let's go."

They spent the next several hours driving in the field. Kate became more comfortable with the truck's feel. She wasn't jerking it anymore when she hit the gas. Jack kept giving her instructions, and soon she was driving as if she knew what she was doing. She didn't think she was ready to hit the road yet, but she was pleased with how far she had come.

"Okay. I think that's enough for today. Let's head back to the house."

Kate put the gear in park and started to open her door.

"No," Jack said. "You're taking us back."

*Is he nuts? What if I drive through his house?* Without arguing, she put the truck back into drive and started for the house. The first tricky part was the gate. She made it through just fine, though. She headed down the same path they had come in on. When the house came into view, she slowed. Her heart was pounding, and she prayed she didn't panic.

"Just pull up over there." Jack pointed to where they had parked before.

*This is it. Brake, Kate. The brake.* She kept repeating that. She drove to where he'd pointed, and she came to a smooth stop. She put the gear in park. Closing her eyes, she let out a huge sigh of relief. They'd made it.

Jack was in his kitchen fixing lunch when Kate came up behind him and put her arms around him. He stopped what he was doing and put his hands over hers. He loved the feel of her. He still couldn't believe she had told him she loved him. He turned around and drew her into his arms. He bent his head and kissed her. This kiss wasn't gentle either. He needed and wanted her. He wanted to make sure she knew how much. He deepened the kiss. He heard her moan. She moved her hands to the front of his shirt. He kissed the corner of her mouth, her chin, and then her jaw. Her hair brushed against his nose. He could smell peaches again.

She reached down and started pulling his shirt out of his jeans. Once it was free, she moved her hand underneath and touched his chest. The feel of her hand on his bare skin was the sexiest thing Jack had ever felt. He'd been with other women. They had had their hands on him, but not one of them had made him feel this way. Now she had both hands on his chest. He moved his leg between her legs. He pressed his erection into her stomach. He moved his hand over her breast. It was soft, round, and full. He squeezed and made her gasp. He started moving his hand lower. He wanted to feel and taste her everywhere. A sound started penetrating through his foggy, hazy mind. The front door was opening and closing. He felt Kate stiffen. He heard footsteps. She heard them too.

"I think we have company," Jack said, and pushed Kate away gently. He was tucking his shirt back in his jeans when his sister walked in.

"Hey, Jack. What happened to—" Avery stopped. She looked at Jack and then at Kate. "Oh," she said, and smiled. "Did I interrupt something?"

Kate said no and Jack said yes at the same time. He looked at Kate and saw her cheeks turning pink. Her hair was tousled, and her lips were swollen. Jack looked back to his sister. She was smirking. "Perfect timing as usual, Avery."

Jack finished tucking his shirt back into his jeans, and then he reached for Kate. She wasn't looking at him or Avery. He lifted her chin and leaned down for a whisper of a kiss. He didn't want her to be embarrassed that they had been caught. He planned on kissing her a lot and didn't give a damn if Avery saw them or not.

When he lifted his head, she was smiling. He gently tucked a strand of hair behind her ear. He then tucked her underneath his shoulder with his arm around her. "What can I do for you, Avery?" he asked impatiently.

"Don't get your panties in a wad." She was not the least embarrassed she had caught them kissing. She winked at Kate. "I brought the mail in." She was holding up a stack of envelopes. "Then I saw your truck, and I knew there was another story I was going to have to hear."

She sat down at one of the barstools, folded her hands, and placed them on the bar. She smiled. "Okay. Let's hear it. And don't leave anything out," she said with enthusiasm.

While Jack finished making lunch, Kate told Avery the story. By the time Kate was done, Avery was laughing so hard, she had tears running down her cheeks. "I would have loved to have seen Jack's face." Avery wiped her tears away.

Kate let out a little laugh. "Well, he did look a little green."

That started another laughing fit from Avery. "He treats that truck like a baby. I told him he should buy another one so it had someone to play with."

Jack turned and glared at her. "Don't you have work or something you need to be doing?"

Avery was still laughing. She stood, walked around the bar, went to Jack, and kissed him on the cheek. "I do." She gave Kate's arm a quick squeeze and was gone.

Jack loved his sister, but sometimes he wanted to put a gag in her mouth. She had made Kate feel comfortable and welcome, though, so he'd put up with her. He looked at Kate and smiled. "Told you. A pistol."

She smiled back. "I like her."

The rest of the day went quickly. Jack gave Kate a tour of the rest of the house. He had four bedrooms. Each had its own bathroom. She asked him what he was going to do with all those rooms, and he told her he liked to plan ahead. He showed her his office. It was a large room with a dark maple desk sitting in front of the only window in the room. Two wingback chairs sat in front of the desk. Bookshelves lined one of the walls. *Also very masculine,* she thought. He told her he tried to spend as little time there as he could. He liked being out working on the ranch instead.

Then they were in the truck again, but Jack was driving. He showed her around his five hundred acres. Kate immediately was lost. She still couldn't believe how big five hundred acres was. They came upon a small river. "It's the Yellowstone River. It's almost seven hundred miles long and flows through three states."

Back at the ranch again, Jack took Kate out to the barn. It was also large. Not as big as the house but still large with a very tall ceiling. Kate could see another level above. Horse stalls took up one side of it. Jack grabbed some apples out of a bin. As they walked, Jack fed each horse an apple out of his palm. When they reached the last stall, Kate knew it belonged to Jack's horse.

The horse stuck her nose over the railing and nuzzled Jack. He laughed and stepped closer. The horse put her nose over his shoulder. Jack was rubbing his hand up and down her neck. "Hey, big girl."

Kate stood back and watched. She didn't know people could form bonds with horses. Clearly, though, this man and his horse had one.

"Come over here, babe. Meet Chestnut." Jack turned to Kate, and she tentatively took a step. Jack smiled, reached for her hand, and pulled her closer. "It's okay. She doesn't bite."

Kate wasn't so sure. She reached up and gave Chestnut a soft pat. When she didn't make any motion to chew her arm off, Kate pet her again. Her hair was soft and slick. *It's nice,* she thought.

"Do you want to feed her?" Jack asked. He held an apple out to her.

She shook her head. "I don't think so." She already had one bad hand. She didn't want another.

Jack, though, reached for her good hand. "Come on. She'll love you for it." He opened Kate's hand and set the apple on her palm. "Hold your hand out. Keep it flat."

She did what he'd told her. Chestnut turned her nose toward Kate. Kate's instinct was telling her to drop her hand, but she kept it steady. Chestnut opened her mouth and snatched the apple out of her hand. Kate squealed, quickly pulled her hand back, and wiped it on her shirt.

Jack laughed. "See? That wasn't so bad." Kate thought the jury was still out on that one, but she shook her head. "It's getting dark now, but maybe next time you could ride her."

Kate wanted to ask him if he remembered the truck incident, but she kept that thought to herself. They were leaving the barn when they heard thunder. Jack looked up at the sky. "Here comes the storm they were talking about earlier." They hadn't taken two steps out of the barn when the first raindrops started falling. Jack reached for Kate's hand. "We're going to make a run for it. Okay?"

She smiled up at him. "I love the rain. Let's just stay here and watch it."

"I don't think so. I don't want you freezing to death. I have plans for you later." He watched her reaction to that statement. He saw her hesitate for just a second, and then she smiled. His breath caught. He squeezed her hand, and they took off.

They reached the house before the downpour really began. Jack started turning on lights. It had been getting darker earlier every night. He glanced over at Kate. She was still standing in the entryway and looking nervous. "Kate," he said softly, "you can come in. We'll go as slowly as you like."

She moved hesitantly into the living room. He didn't move toward her. He was afraid she'd run if he did. Instead he headed for the kitchen. "You hungry?"

*I'll make her dinner. Then we'll see what happens after that.* He hoped she was ready, but he would wait if she wasn't.

Not waiting for her to answer, he started taking pans out of the cabinet. He would make spaghetti. That was simple and easy. He had just filled a pot with water when the lights went out.

# 15

**D**amn. He headed back to the living room. He could make out the furniture shapes, but he didn't see Kate. "Kate?" He frowned. There was no answer. He moved to the center of the room. *Where is she?* "Kate?" he said louder.

The lights flickered back on. He looked around for her and blinked in the bright lights. Then he saw her. She was in a corner of the room sitting with her knees up to her chest. Her gun was out and pointed at him. He froze. *What the hell?*

"Kate, what are you doing?" He didn't move.

She wasn't hearing him. She seemed locked in some sort of terror. His heart twisted. Her face was pale. It was like looking at a ghost. Carefully, he took a step toward her. "Kate, listen to me." She was looking at him, but Jack didn't think she was seeing him. "It's Jack." He took another step. "Kate, it's okay. You're safe." He took another step. "It's Jack." He kept repeating each sentence with each step. When he reached her, he slowly bent down but kept his eye on the gun. He didn't touch her. "Kate, honey, you're scaring me."

Her eyes blinked. "Jack?"

He let out the breath he had been holding. "Yeah, babe. It's me."

Her face crumbled, and the gun fell to the floor. He reached for her and brought her in close. Her shoulders were shaking. *My God. What happened to her?* He felt helpless. Not knowing how to soothe her, he just kept holding her.

He didn't know how long they stayed that way before her tears stopped. She leaned away from him and wiped her tears. "I'm sorry. You probably think I'm crazy."

He reached up to wipe away another tear. "I don't think you're crazy. I think you're scared."

He stood and picked her up. Carrying her over to the couch, he sat down with her on his lap. "Can you tell me what happened? Why are you scared?" He stroked her arm, and he felt her trembling. Picking her up again, he set her down on the couch beside him. She started to protest, but he said, "I'm not going anywhere. I'm going to get a blanket and something for you to drink."

Not wanting to leave her alone long, he rushed into his bedroom and grabbed the blanket off the end of the bed. He noticed she was still shivering and staring off into space when he returned.

He gently placed the blanket over her. He then went to the bar and poured her a drink. He came back and handed the glass to her. When she took it, he picked her up and set her back down on his lap. She hadn't taken a sip yet. He took the glass and brought it to her lips. "Take a drink."

She took a sip and started coughing. When she had the coughing under control, she handed it back to him. "I really don't drink."

He pushed it back to her. "Just a couple more sips. It'll warm you up."

She took another drink and didn't cough this time. When she was done, he took the glass and downed the rest. He needed warming up too. He'd been shaken to the core when he saw her sitting in that corner with a look of terror on her face. He wanted to know what had happened to her, but a part of him was afraid. If he wanted to help her, though, he needed to know.

"Can you tell me what happened now?" He held her tightly.

She rested her head on his shoulder. She took a shaky breath. "Two years ago I was living in Portland, Oregon. I had a life there. It was a quiet life, but I liked it. I had a good job, which I loved, working in a bookstore. I was going to school. I had an apartment. It was home for me. Then one day it all came crashing down."

Kissing her forehead, he asked gently, "What happened?"

"*He* happened."

Jack tensed. He felt her shudder, and then she snuggled closer to him. He tightened his arms around her. She told him about the book she was reading called *The Purple Rose* and then having purple roses left at her doorstep. She told him about Nick and then going to the police. "That's when I met Paine."

Jack looked down at her. "He's a cop?"

She nodded. "They all are. Ben, Jake, and Bill." Jack nodded. "One night I was at work. I was getting ready to close when the lights went out."

Jack hoped his body didn't show any reaction. He wasn't sure he was ready to hear the rest of this. *Get a grip, Jack. She lived it. You sure as hell can hear it.*

"He grabbed me from behind and pressed me up against the wall." Jack suddenly understood her reaction when they'd been at the waterfall. She was breathing harder now. "He wanted to know if I liked his surprises." Jack swore. "That's all he did that night, but he told me he would be back."

"If you're not ready, Kate, you don't have to do this."

She shook her head. "Yes, I do. You need to know what you're getting yourself into. Because it gets worse."

*Oh God. Did he rape her?* Jack felt ill.

"One night I went to the bar where Nick worked. I was looking for him, but he wasn't there. A man tried hitting on me, and he grabbed my arm." Jack flinched. "Nothing happened. I told him no and left. The man was found with his throat slit a couple of days later. A purple rose and a note were pinned to his chest. The note said, 'Kate, have you noticed me yet?'"

Jack balled his hands into fists. "Son of a bitch."

She pushed the blanket away and scooted off his lap. She stood. He tried reaching for her. "It's okay. I just need to walk." He let her go. "After that, Paine and the other guys were with me constantly. Nothing happened for two months." She then told Jack about the protection detail being pulled and how the guys still tried to be with her on their own time. *No wonder she's close with them. They tried to protect her even when they weren't on the job.* Jack was starting to like these guys.

"The first night without their protection, he came for me again." Jack stood. He wanted to reach for her but he stayed where he was.

He was afraid to hear what came next. "He was at the bookstore. He had me on the ground. Holding me down." Tears were coming down Kate's cheeks. Jack couldn't take it anymore. He went to her. He put his arms around her. Kate buried her head in his chest. "I tried to fight him, Jack, but he had my arms pinned down. He…"

Jack leaned away from her. "Kate, you don't have to tell me." *I'm going to kill this son of a bitch. Hunt him down and kill him.*

"He did hurt me."

Jack brought her back into his arms. "Kate, sit on the couch with me. Let me hold you." He needed to hold her and not let go.

She stepped away. "No. I want to tell you. So you understand." Her tears were gone, and she sounded calmer now. "He warned me if I didn't stay away from Paine and the others, he would hurt them." She turned to look at him. "He said he would know if they didn't stay away."

Jack was thinking that over. *How could he know? He couldn't watch her every minute of every day. He would need inside information.* Then it hit him. "He's a cop."

He looked at Kate. She was nodding. "That's what we think." Jack swore. *A cop?* Kate was pacing again. "After that he handcuffed me to the radiator and left." She fell onto the couch.

Jack sat next to her and took her hands into his. "What did you do?" he asked gently.

Tears were in her eyes again. "I couldn't let them get hurt because of me. I didn't tell them I was leaving. They wouldn't have let me. So I just left." She sniffled. "They still don't know where I am." She laughed. "Even though Paine asks me every time we talk."

Putting his arms around her again, he rested his chin on her head. "Kate, I'm sorry." He rubbed her back absently. "I'm sorry you went through that. What you're still going through. And on your own." He leaned away from her and lifted her chin so she could look at him. "Kate, you're not alone anymore. I'm here with you, and I'll always be with you. I'm not letting you go." He hugged her tightly.

*God, I love him.* She didn't know she could love like that. She loved Paine and the others, but this was something different. It was a strong, powerful, all-consuming love. It scared her. *What if something happens to him because of me? I can't—won't—let that happen.* She had thought she could make this work somehow, but telling the horrible story again, she didn't see how. *What if he finds me with Jack? What would he do to him? Am I willing to take that chance?* She knew she would have to leave soon. Her heart would shatter into a million pieces, but she would leave to protect him.

She wanted him to love her for one night, though. She just needed one night to help her get through the rest of the dark, lonely nights. Then she would leave. She still hadn't told him every-thing, though. If she wanted that one night, she was going to have to tell him.

Summoning all her courage, she pulled away. She looked at him and hoped the love she felt for him showed in her eyes. "Jack, I want us to make love. I love you, and I need you."

His eyes turned even darker with desire. He started to reach for her, but she put her hand on his chest to stop him. "Babe, what is it?" He frowned down at her. "You know I love you and how much I want you."

She looked down at her lap. She had to tell him. "I told you he hurt me." She was having trouble breathing. She took his hand and squeezed it tight. "But I didn't tell you how he hurt me."

She felt his whole body tense. She let go of his hand and started to unbutton her shirt. Her hands were shaking so badly, it took her several tries to undo each button. He was watching her with so much intensity. Kate's hands started to shake worse. She was at the last but-ton. She hesitated. Now that it was time, she didn't know if she could do it. Jack put his hand on her leg. "Kate, it won't matter. Whatever it is, it won't matter."

The love she saw in his eyes gave her the courage she needed. Kate opened her shirt. She couldn't look at him. "He said he wanted to mark me so no other man would want me." When he didn't say anything, she looked up at him. Her heart sank to her stomach. All the desire and yearning were gone. Instead she haw hatred, anger, and disgust.

With tears in her eyes, she closed her shirt. "I know the scars are ugly," she choked out. Her throat felt as if it were closing. "I understand."

She started to get up off the couch, but he grabbed her roughly. Startled, she tried to pull away. "God, Kate. I'm sorry."

He quickly let her go. He stood and walked to the window. Kate watched him. He just stood there staring out the window. *He doesn't want me anymore,* Kate thought bitterly. *He can't even look at me.* She knew the scars were grotesque. *He* had wanted to hurt her. He said he was making sure nobody else would want her. It had worked.

She thought Jack had wanted her. He had said it wouldn't matter. He had lied. She was not going to let him see how much he had hurt her. She would leave with her pride intact. She would cry when she was alone.

*Jack can go screw himself. If he can't deal with it, then he's not the man I thought he was.* She stood. "Fuck you, Jack." She turned and headed for the door. *I will not cry,* she told herself.

She had her hand on the doorknob when she felt Jack's hands on her shoulders. He spun her around. "Where the hell do you think you're going?"

She tried twisting out of his hands, but he wouldn't let her go. "Let go of me!" she yelled. She was slapping at him, trying to get free.

"Damn it, Kate. Calm down."

She was angry, sad, and humiliated. She just wanted out of there. She tried to knee him in the groin, but he twisted away. She stepped down on his foot hard. She heard him growl in pain, but he didn't loosen his hold on her. She kept slapping at him. He cursed and grabbed both her wrists. "Kate, stop! Babe, please stop."

She stopped. She was breathing hard, and then she burst into tears. Kate felt herself being picked up and carried over to the couch. Jack sat down and put her on his lap. He was rubbing her back, kissing her head, and telling her everything was going to be all right. She cried until she had nothing left.

She raised her head and wiped her tears away. She didn't look at him. She tried getting off his lap, but he tightened his hold on her. "Please, Kate. Stay here," he said desperately.

She looked at him. She thought she saw fear in his eyes. She wanted to reach up and touch his face, but she didn't. She couldn't bring herself to do it. Instead she sat silently.

She felt him take a breath. "I handled that badly." Kate didn't say anything. "This isn't about the scars, Kate." She peeked up at him. He was looking down at her. "You know what those scars mean to me?" Kate shook her head. "They mean survival. It means you survived."

She pulled away from him. "I know they're ugly."

He pulled her back. "Kate, you're beautiful inside and out. You have to know I think you're beautiful."

Kate could feel tears coming again. She thought she was cried out. He was looking at her with tenderness and regret. "I don't understand. I thought you were disgusted," she said with ragged breaths.

He hugged her and rested his chin on her head. "I guess I was disgusted." Kate flinched. "But not by you, Kate." Jack picked her up and gently set her down on the couch next to him. He turned her so they were face-to-face. "I'm disgusted somebody would do that to you." He jaws clenched. "I can't stand the thought of somebody hurting you."

As if he couldn't stand sitting anymore, Jack jumped up from the couch and started pacing. Kate watched him. With every step, he seemed to get angrier. "I want to find this bastard and kill him."

He stopped and looked at her. Kate sucked in a breath. His face was a mask of anger. His eyes looked like black pools of water. His lips were bared back over his teeth. Kate wasn't afraid of Jack, though. She stood and walked over to him. She took his hands into hers. "Jack," she whispered softly. He seemed to stare at nothing. "Jack," Kate said again. He looked down at her and then at her hands holding his. She saw his anger start to fade.

She reached up and put her hand on his cheek. He put his hand over hers, turned his head, and kissed her palm. "You're right, Jack. I did survive. And I don't want to waste any more time waiting. I've put my life on hold, waiting for this to be over." Her heart was pounding. "It might never be over." Jack tried to interrupt, but Kate stopped him. "But I want to start living again. I want to be with you, Jack. I want you to love me."

Taking one of her hands, he started pulling her down the hallway toward his bedroom. "I'm going to show you, Kate, just how beautiful you really are."

*He's behind her. She can hear his feet pounding on the concrete. Run. She can't run. Her feet feel as if they have cement blocks attached to them. He's gaining on her. Her heart is thrashing in her chest. She keeps running, but she is moving in slow motion. She can hear his breathing now. He's close.*

*She turns when she feels him grab her shirt. She sees the knife. Blood covers it. Her blood. He tackles her to the ground. He is leaning over her. He is a faceless shadow looking down at her. "Kate, don't you know by now you're mine?" She sees him lift the knife over his head. He is swinging it down toward her chest.*

Kate sat up in bed and screamed. She was breathing hard, and her heart was pounding. Sweat covered her. She heard someone talking to her. "Kate, babe, it's Jack. You're safe."

Her hands covered her face. *Will these nightmares ever go away?* She felt Jack put his arms around her. She leaned into him. She was with Jack. She was safe. "I'm sorry, Jack. I haven't had a nightmare in a while. I was hoping they had gone away," she said when her breathing was under control.

Jack held her tighter. "It's okay. I'm not surprised you have nightmares." He leaned away so he could look at her. "Have you talked to someone about them? A professional?"

Kate was twisting the sheets in her hands. She suddenly realized she was sitting there naked. She looked at Jack's bare chest. He was all skin and muscles. He had a patch of chest hair running down the middle and traveling down below the sheets. She averted her eyes and tried to pull the sheet up to cover herself. Jack stopped her.

He helped her lie back on the pillow and started kissing her scars. "Kate, you don't have to hide your scars from me." He kissed each one. "You have to know you're beautiful. And I love you."

Kate's heart melted and broke at the same time. *How am I going to leave this man?* She moved so she could see his eyes. He leaned away and rested on his elbow.

"I know it's silly to cover myself after…" She felt her cheeks grow warm. "After what we did last night." She looked away. It had been the most incredible night of her life. She hadn't known sex could be like that. *Maybe it was just incredible because it was with Jack.* She was going to have to tell him she had to leave.

"Kate, look at me."

She lifted her eyes to his. Amusement was dancing there. "Are you laughing at me?" She frowned.

He did laugh then. "No, babe. I'm not laughing. I just think you're adorable." He was tracing his finger along the top of the sheet and over her chest and scars.

Her breathing became shallow. She felt the heat between them. There was always so much heat. She put her hand around his neck and pulled him down. He moved his lips over her jawline to where her neck met her shoulder. Goose bumps covered her skin. "I love kissing you, Kate." His lips were making their way back to hers. "I love you." He whispered this before covering her mouth with his. Kate forgot all about her nightmare and about telling him she was leaving.

# 16

**"W**here is she?" he screamed in his apartment.

He didn't care who heard him. He needed Kate. He'd done everything for her, and she still hadn't come back. What was it going to take to get her to come back?

She had to know about the women. Those women died because of her. It was those cop friends of hers who were holding the information back. Did they really think they were protecting her?

He didn't know how much longer he could hold out without Kate. She was like a drug to him. She was all he thought about. He had to think of a different plan to get her to come back. He had to think of something that would make her want to come back.

He suddenly knew what he had to do. She would come back for the same reason she had left—to protect her cop friends.

He left his apartment with a plan in mind. Sometimes he was so clever, he scared himself. He had to scold himself a little for not thinking of it before. This was Kate's fault. She was clouding his mind. When she came back, he would make sure she was punished. First, though, he had to put his plan in motion.

He cruised in his car until he found the right one. She wouldn't be perfect like Kate, but she would just have to do.

He saw her coming out of a bar. She had long brown hair, but that was as close to Kate as she was going to get. She didn't have the same build as Kate, and she wasn't nearly as beautiful as she was. But he was too impatient to wait for someone better.

He parked his car across the street from where she was walking and started to follow her. She wore some skimpy dress that barely covered her ass. Her shoes were red high heels. *Whore.* She was weaving back and forth as if drunk. She wouldn't be the challenge he had hoped for, but he was eager to get Kate back.

He watched as she turned the corner. He hurriedly crossed the street and kept an eye on her. She had no idea he was behind her. *Stupid bitch.* They were all so stupid. He had been following her for a couple of minutes when she stopped suddenly. He stopped. She was just standing there. *What is she doing?* Then he watched as she slowly turned around. He didn't move.

"Hey, asshole. Are you following me?" he heard her slur.

"Yes. I am."

"Why?"

He smiled. "Because I'm going to kill you."

She kept looking at him. Then she started to move backward. Suddenly she turned and started running. He knew she wouldn't get very far in those shoes. He started after her. He was surprised how far ahead she got. He moved a little faster. He saw her turn into an alley. Didn't the bitch know the alley was the last place she should go? He chuckled. It was just too damn easy.

When he turned into the alley, she was gone. He started moving slowly through the alley. "You can't hide from me." He moved farther along. "You might as well come out." He slowly moved toward a large trash can. "I want you to know this is all Kate's fault. She's the reason you have to die tonight." When he reached the trash can, he peeked around it. She wasn't there. He moved on. "I do appreciate the game of hide-and-seek, though. You've made this more exciting than I was expecting."

He heard something move behind him. He whipped around and saw the bitch trying to run from the alley. He ran after her. He could hear her crying. She kept looking back over her shoulder while running. That was a mistake. She tripped and landed hard on the concrete. When he saw she wasn't moving, he slowed his pace. He took his time getting to her. It was too bad the chase hadn't lasted longer. When he reached her, she was lying there, looking up at him. "Please," she begged.

"Please, what?"

"Please don't kill me," she said through sobs.

He laughed. They always begged in the end.

Kate woke to a ringing in her ears. *What is that? Where am I?* She was lying on her stomach in bed—Jack's bed. She smiled. Then she frowned. It was the damn ringing again.

She turned her head and looked for Jack. The bed was empty. She could see the imprint of his hand on the pillow. She heard the shower running. She still couldn't believe what had happened the night before. Several times. She smiled. The first time had been gentle and tender. He had made her feel as cherished as a porcelain doll. Then, after her nightmare, she had gone wild. She had been so eager for him, it scared her, and he had been just as eager and demanding. She had lost all her inhibitions. Her face warmed just thinking about it.

The ringing interrupted her thoughts. *The phone. My phone.* Kate sat up quickly and covered herself with the sheet. She reached for her phone on the nightstand. She yawned and answered. "Hello, Paine."

"Hey, kiddo. How are you doing? Sounds as if I woke you."

Kate scooted back on the bed and sat cross-legged. *Might as well get comfortable,* she thought. "No. I'm up. How are you doing?" She could hear his chair squeaking. She smiled. He really needed to oil that thing or get a new one.

"I'm putting you on speakerphone, Kate." She sat up straighter at these words. "The rest of the guys are here."

Kate felt a little exposed talking to them with only a sheet on even though they couldn't see her. She looked around for her clothes, but she didn't see them right away. *Oh well,* Kate thought. *Nothing I can do about it now.* Whatever Paine was holding back, she was going to have to hear without her clothes on. She felt a flutter of nerves.

"Okay, Kate. We're all on the line now."

"Hi, guys." She couldn't sit anymore. She stood, wrapped the sheet tighter around her, and started pacing.

"Hi, Kate," they all said at once.

Jake didn't make a joke. She knew whatever it was must be serious. "So, Paine, are you ready to tell me what's going on yet?" Her calm voice surprised her even though she felt like she was ready to jump out of her skin.

"Kate, honey, you need to tell me where you are."

Kate laughed. "Paine, how many times are we going to have this conversation?"

Ben spoke up. "Kate, I think you should tell us where you are."

Kate stopped pacing. "What happened?" She started shaking. This couldn't be good.

"Kate, this is Bill. You need to let Paine come to you, and he can explain everything to you."

Kate was shaking her head, even though they couldn't see her. "No. It's not safe. He'll know. I won't let him hurt you guys."

"Dammit, Kate. I told you before we can take care of ourselves," Jake said angrily.

"I know you guys can take care of yourselves, but if something did happen, I couldn't live with that." *Don't they understand?*

"Kate, what I need to tell you, I don't want to tell you over the phone," Paine said hurriedly.

Kate's heart was racing. *What's happened? How bad can it be? Should I take the risk of telling Paine where I am?* Then another thought occurred to her. *What about Jack? What if Paine led the stalker to Wyoming? He could hurt Jack. Or Avery.* She definitely couldn't live with that. "Paine, I don't think that's a good idea." She hesitated. "I'm not alone anymore," she said quietly.

They didn't say anything. Kate waited. She had them speechless. It would have been funny in another situation. "Paine?"

After a few silent moments they all started at once.

"What the hell does that mean?"

"Who's there with you?"

"Is it the waterfall guy?"

"Everybody, shut up!" Paine yelled. "Kate, do you mean Jack?" Paine asked more calmly.

Kate sighed. She had known she would have to tell them eventually. She just hadn't counted on it being quite so soon. She had wanted it to be just her and Jack for the little time she had left with him. She should have known this nightmare would interfere. "Yes, Paine. It's Jack."

Turning, she saw Jack standing in the bathroom doorway with nothing but a towel around his waist. Her breath caught in her throat. She couldn't help but stare. She had seen every inch of him last night. *The way he's standing in the door—with his bare chest—well, there should be a law.* He was gorgeous. His hair was still wet from his shower, and his face was freshly shaved. He was listening.

"I love him, Paine," she said, looking at Jack. "It's not just about me anymore."

Kate watched as a smile spread across Jack's face. He started moving toward her. He never broke eye contact. He kept coming. Kate watched him moving toward her. He looked like a lion ready to pounce on its prey. He looked as if he wanted to devour her.

Someone was yelling in her ear. *Paine.* She had forgotten about Paine. She put her hand up to stop Jack. She couldn't concentrate with him around. She turned her back to him.

Paine was saying something. "I'm sorry, Paine. What did you say?"

"Kate, I'm happy for you. I really am. But that doesn't change anything. I need to come see you," Paine said impatiently.

"I'm not going to tell you. I can't risk it." She didn't want to tell Paine she was leaving yet. She needed to tell Jack first.

"Dammit, Kate. You not telling me isn't an option anymore. Tell me where you are."

Kate sighed. "How many times are we going to do this? I told you I'm not—"

"He's killing women, Kate."

Kate felt the blood leave her face. Her heart was pounding so hard it, felt as if it were coming out of her chest. Sensing something wrong, Jack was beside her with his arm around her waist.

"How do you know it's him?" she asked in a ragged voice. *It can't be about me. Not again.* Deep down, though, she knew it was.

"Kate, I'm sorry, honey. I didn't mean to blurt it out like that."

She started shaking. "How do you know it's him, Paine?"

"Kate, just tell me where you are, and I'll come."

"Dammit, Paine. Tell me."

Jack was standing in front of her now. Worry covered his face. "What's going on, babe?" he asked.

Kate shook her head and leaned in to him. She should never have started something she couldn't finish. She didn't regret it, though. She would keep the memory with her always. She had gotten her one night. Kate pulled away. She knew she was going to have to be strong to leave Jack. She didn't want him anywhere near this nightmare.

Paine was talking again. "Kate, he's leaving notes."

Kate would have collapsed where she stood if Jack hadn't grabbed her and set her on the bed. "What do they say?" she asked in a shaky voice. She already knew, though. She didn't need Paine to say it.

"Please," Paine begged.

"Kate, it's Bill." Even Bill sounded rattled. "I know this is hard, but I want you to listen to me." Kate was too numb to answer. "Kate, are you there?"

*He's killing again for me. Why? I've been gone. I left. Why is he killing?* She found her voice. "I'm here, Bill. Just tell me what the notes say."

"The first one said, 'Kate, have you noticed me yet?'" Paine said evenly.

"First?" Kate was afraid to ask. "How many?"

"If you would just tell me where you are, we can talk about this."

"How many, Paine?" Kate yelled.

Paine let out a breath. "There have been six in the last six months."

"Oh God. Oh God." Kate started rocking back and forth. She couldn't breathe.

Jack was on his knees in front of her. Fear was on his face. "Kate, babe, talk to me. What's going on?"

"I can't breathe." She stood up and looked around frantically. She didn't know what to do. She could feel a panic attack coming. She needed air. She couldn't get enough air. "Jack, I need air. I can't breathe."

Jack stood in front of her and was holding her shoulders. "Kate, look at me." Kate tried to focus. "That's it, Kate. Just look at me. I'm here. I love you." She saw Jack. "That's right. I'm right here."

Kate felt air going into her lungs. She could breathe. Jack was here. She was not alone. Her breathing started returning to normal. Jack was here. She looked at him and gave him a small smile. His face relaxed. "Hi, babe."

"Hi," she whispered.

"You're okay now," Jack said.

She realized she was still holding the phone to her ear. She heard Paine talking. "Honey, are you okay?"

She felt a tear run down her cheek. She hadn't even known she was crying. "I'm fine now." She wiped the tears away. Kate turned her attention back to the phone. "Why didn't you tell me, Paine?" She thought she had done the right thing by leaving. She had wanted to protect Paine and the others, but now six women were dead. "You should have told me. Why didn't you tell me?" she said, choking on her words.

"Kate, I wanted to tell you, but I didn't know if it was the right thing to do. You seemed safe, and I was afraid you would want to come back. Even though I want you home, I thought you were safer where you were. But now I don't know."

Kate could hear frustration in his voice. She understood, but he still should have told her. "What does that mean? 'Now you don't know'?" Paine didn't answer. "You might as well tell me the rest," she said in a monotone voice.

"He's escalating, Kate," Paine said tersely.

"What do you mean?"

"The notes. Each note has been different."

"Dammit. Tell me what they say." Kate's control had snapped.

"The second note said, 'Why hasn't she noticed me yet?' The third note said, 'Where is she? She has to notice me.' The fourth one said, 'When will she notice me?' And the fifth one said, 'I will make her notice me.' It's the last note, though, that has me worried, Kate."

Kate felt her breathing changing. She was taking deep breaths when she felt Jack's arm come around her waist. She looked at him. He was there. "What did the last note say?" She kept her eyes on Jack.

Paine hesitated slightly. "It said, 'If she won't notice me, I'll make her notice them,'" Paine said in a rush.

Kate understood immediately what the last note meant. *No!* "He's talking about you. And Bill and Jake and Ben."

"Kate, listen to me. We're not worried about us. We're worried about you. I don't want him to use us against you. He's just trying to draw you out. Make you come back."

"You're right, Paine. But it is time for me to come back. Six women are dead." Kate dropped to the floor. She had to go back. She couldn't hide from *him* anymore. Her hand covered her eyes. She had to go back.

Jack couldn't stand it. He grabbed the phone out of Kate's hand. "Paine, right?" he asked stiffly.

"You must be Jack."

"That's right. Mind telling me what the hell's going on?"

"Put Kate back on the phone. Now."

"I don't think so, asshole." He felt Kate put her hand on his chest. He looked down at her. She was pale, and her eyes were red from crying. She did look calmer, though. She didn't look as if she were going to break into a thousand pieces. She had scared him, and he didn't know what to do. He did know one thing, though. He needed to know what was going on.

"It's okay, Jack. Let me have the phone."

*Like hell. This Paine guy has upset her enough.* He was shaking his head and not letting go of the phone.

"I'm okay now. Please let me talk to Paine."

He kissed her on the forehead and handed the phone back to her. "I'm right here, babe."

He stayed close to her. He could feel her tension, but she was holding it together. He didn't know all the facts, but women were dead, and there was something to do with notes. He frowned at her next words.

"I'm coming back, Paine. I can be there tomorrow."

*No way in hell am I letting her leave.* He grabbed the phone from her again and put it to his ear. "She'll call you back." He heard Paine yelling when he hit the end button.

Looking back at Kate, he could see she was angry.

"What the hell are you doing?" She tried to grab her phone from him, but he held it out of her reach. She grabbed for it again. "Jack, give me the damn phone. I have to call Paine back." She blew out a breath of frustration.

"I'm not letting you go back, Kate," he announced calmly. He knew he sounded like an ass, but he was afraid. He was afraid she was leaving him and even more afraid she was going back to face a monster.

"I'm going back, Jack. You can't stop me," she said stubbornly.

Taking her hands in his, he pulled her down to sit on the bed. "Tell me what's happened. We can figure this out together." *No matter what, she isn't doing this without me.*

"Six women have been killed because of me."

Jack heard the guilt in her voice. "Kate, look at me." She turned her head toward him. Those blue eyes pierced his heart. She looked so vulnerable. "This isn't your fault. It's that sick, twisted bastard's fault."

Kate was shaking her head. "You don't understand. He's leaving notes. Notes with my name on them. How is that not my fault? I thought I left to protect Paine and the others, but deep down I think I left because I was scared. For myself. And now women are dead."

Jack took her in his arms. His heart broke a little more. "Babe, you had every right to be scared. To still be scared. But you left the protection of four cops who quite frankly sound as if they would rip the head off a snake for you." She smiled. "You went out alone so they would be safe. From where I'm sitting, that sounds like courage." *Doesn't she know how strong she is?* "Now tell me what the notes said." He listened as Kate explained each note.

"The last note. I think he's going to go after Paine and the rest of the guys."

"It's okay, babe. They know how to take care of themselves."

"That's what they keep telling me."

"We'll figure it out. Whatever needs to be done, we'll do it together," Jack said fervently. "Because I love you, and I want to be with you through this. No matter what."

She lifted her head. "I don't want anything to happen to you."

He couldn't help himself. He lowered his head and kissed her gently on the mouth. She kissed him back. *God, I love her.* He couldn't let her leave. She was his. He broke the kiss. He had an idea, but he didn't think she was going to like it. Jack picked her up to sit on his lap.

She put her arms around his neck. "I have to go back. I can't let more women die because of me. We talked about this. You said you wouldn't try to stop me when it was time to leave."

Jack remembered that conversation. He hadn't actually made any promises about stopping her from leaving, but he wasn't going to point that out right now. He didn't want to make her angry. He wanted her thinking straight when he presented his idea.

"I'm not going to stop you." He felt her relax. "Because I'm going with you."

She jumped up from his lap before he could stop her. He stood too. Kate was pacing again. She stopped and looked at him. "I'm not doing this, Jack. You can't come with me." She went back to pacing.

Jack went over to her and reached for her hand. "You must not think very much of me if you think I'm the kind of man who would let the woman he loves go to face this alone."

"That's not fair." Kate pulled her hand from his. "Do you think I would let the man I love come with me and put his life in danger?"

"Do you remember I was cop? I can take of myself."

Kate whirled around to face him. "This guy has killed people, Jack. People I don't even know. What do you think he would do to you if he knew what you meant to me?"

Jack's anger slipped away. "Kate, I can't let you go by yourself. I can't stand by and wait for you to come back. I'm not built that way."

Kate went to him. "What about your ranch?" *There she goes again,* he thought. *Worrying about the damn ranch.* "I don't know how long this is going to take."

"I have Avery and Shane here. They can take care of things while I'm gone. If I have to, I'll hire somebody to help them." He lifted her chin to look her in the eye. "One way or another, I'm coming."

Kate sighed. "I don't think you understand." She took a deep breath. "I'm not going back just so he'll know I'm there. I'm going back to set a trap." She took his hand into hers. "I can't live like this anymore. Hiding. Being scared of my own shadow. I have to end this. I hope you can understand."

Jack took her in his arms. "I don't like it, but I understand it." He leaned away so he could look at her. "That's why I'm going. I have to be there, Kate. I know you have Paine and the others, but I need to be there too. I hope you can understand."

Kate smiled. "I don't like it, but I can understand it," she repeated. Then she pulled away. "Paine's definitely not going to like it."

Jack snorted. "I don't give a rat's ass if Paine doesn't like it."

Kate walked back to him and frowned. "Paine and the others are very important to me. They put their lives on hold for me. To protect me." Jack started to interrupt. Kate stopped him. "I want you to try to get along with them. I love you, but they mean a lot to me too."

Jack pulled her into his arms again. "I know. I promise I will be on my best behavior." He kissed the top of her head and then let go of her. "You better call Paine back before he has a heart attack."

Kate nodded. "I'm going to get dressed first. I don't know if I can do this dressed only in a sheet."

"I don't know, babe. I'm pretty sure you could convince me to do anything if you were dressed only in a sheet."

Kate was shaking her head when she walked into the bathroom, but Jack didn't miss the pink hue on her cheeks. Jack suddenly had another idea. He didn't want to tell Kate yet, though. She would fret and worry. He needed to talk to Paine.

"Kate, are you crazy?" Paine said.

Kate had known he wasn't going to like it. She and Jack were sitting on the couch in the living room. Jack was practically glued to her side, trying to listen to Paine. He was still talking. "We don't know anything about this guy. I know you care for him, Kate, but it's not a good idea."

She could feel Jack tensing. She gave him a warning look. Jack scowled, sat back on the couch, and put his legs on the coffee table. *Great,* Kate thought. *Now I have both of them upset. Might as well go for broke.* "Paine, you don't have much of a choice. It's my decision. He's coming."

She heard Jack snicker behind her. She ignored him. Now Kate tensed. She knew Paine would eventually do what she wanted. She just wanted what? His blessing? His cooperation? She didn't know what she wanted, but it was important that Paine be okay with this. She waited for him to say something.

A few silent moments passed before Paine said anything. "Okay. He's coming." Kate let out her breath. "But I want to talk to him."

Kate frowned and turned to look at Jack. "Why?" She didn't know if that was a great idea. Jack put his feet on the ground and sat up next to her.

"That's the deal, Kate. He can come, but I want to talk to him."

*How bad could it be? They will have to deal with each other sometime.* She shrugged and said, "Okay. Here he is."

Paine waited for Jack to come on the line. Paine didn't know if this was a good idea, but he needed to get a feel for this man. If he was coming back with Kate, he needed to know he wasn't going to put her life or his men's lives in danger. He could be a real wimp, Paine figured, though he didn't see Kate with a man who couldn't take care of himself. Paine looked around at his men. They were looking at him as if he'd lost his mind.

"This is Jack."

*Well,* Paine thought, *at least he doesn't sound like a wimp.* Looking away from his men, he spoke into the phone. "Jack, I'm Mark Paine. You can call me Paine."

"Okay."

"Cut the bullshit, Jack! I want to know your name. Your full name."

There was a moment of hesitation. "Jack Rivers." Then he heard, "Ouch. Okay. Okay, babe." There was another pause. "And it's nice to meet you."

Paine felt himself smiling. This guy had it bad. "So, I hear you're coming back with Kate."

"You have a problem with that?"

Paine heard the challenge in Jack's voice and approved. "It's seems this is what Kate wants. So it doesn't matter if I have a problem with it or not."

"Nope. Doesn't matter."

Paine let out a frustrated breath. He didn't want to get into a pissing match with this guy. "Look, I know you care for Kate."

Before he could go on, Jack interrupted him. "I love her. I care about what happens to her as much as you guys. She's told me what you guys did for her. Protecting her. For that I thank you. I was a cop for ten years. I know how to take care of myself." Paine sensed he wasn't done. "And I want to get this guy. I want to get him badly."

Paine knew how he felt. "Fine. We'll need a couple of days to put things together here. We need to find a safe place for her to stay."

"She wants to set a trap."

The news didn't surprise Paine. He knew Kate. People were getting hurt. She would do whatever it took to stop it. "I suppose you can't talk her out of this?"

Jack gave a humorless laugh. "Yeah. Right. You know how many times I had to ask her out before she said yes? She's stubborn."

Paine smiled. "Do you know how many times I've asked her where she is?"

"Besides," Jack said, "I have a new plan I want to talk to you about."

Paine and Jack spent the next forty-five minutes coming up with a plan of action. It seemed they had both agreed to call a truce. If Paine was being honest, he actually liked the guy. Jack's plan was pretty good. He seemed to know what he was talking about. That still didn't mean he wasn't going to check up on him.

He hung up with Jack without first running the plan by Kate. He was probably going to get an earful for that. He smiled. He'd let Jack deal with that.

Paine looked up to talk with his men. "What do you think?"

Bill spoke first. "I think it will work, but we're going to have to be damn careful how we play this."

Ben wasn't so sure. "What about this Jack guy? We don't know anything about him. Can he do his part?"

Paine nodded. "He says he was a cop. I'll check him out, but he sounds solid." Leaning back in his chair, he looked at all them. "Well? Are we doing this or not?"

They looked at each other. Coming to a silent agreement, they nodded.


He watched them through the glass window. They were all huddled around the desk. They were so stupid. He was right there under their noses, and they had no idea. Sometimes he wanted to walk up to them and say, "Hi. Looking for me?" That would show them how stupid they were. He would never do that, though. He wanted Kate more.

Something was happening. He could feel it. He knew they had to be talking to Kate. They were all in there. He tried moving closer to the door. He couldn't be seen. They would suspect something. He picked up a file on a nearby desk and headed for the hallway.

When he was several feet from the door, he opened the file and pretended to be reading it. The door was slightly ajar. He could still only catch every other word or so. He needed to get closer. *Is it worth the risk?* If he was ever going to be with his Kate again, he was going to have to take some risks. It had been so long since he had touched her or smelled her. His beautiful Kate. Inching closer and still pretending to be engrossed in the file, he listened. The blond one was talking. "Who's this Jack guy?"

He frowned. *Jack? Who the hell is Jack?* Maybe they weren't talking with Kate earlier. He started to walk away but stopped when he heard Kate's name. "Kate says she's in love with him."

*She's in love? No!* This had to be a mistake. His Kate wouldn't do that to him. She was a good girl. She couldn't be in love with anyone. She was his. Fury ran through his whole body. He wanted to ram his fist into the wall. He took deep breaths to calm himself. They were still talking.

"She's coming back, and he's coming too."

Then he heard yelling. "We don't know anything about this guy. How does she know she can trust him?"

The one in charge was yelling back. "She says she trusts him with her life! What do you want me to do? I can't talk her out of this. She loves him."

*That bitch! She's just like the rest of them. Whores. They're all whores. She is going to pay for this. Dearly.* By the time he was done with her, she would be begging him to kill her. He wouldn't kill her right away, though. He was going to have his fun first. Then maybe he would kill her. He had another idea. He would kill her boyfriend first in front of her. He'd make her beg for his life.

Out of the corner of his eye, he saw movement. The door was opening. He moved down the hallway to the next office. He was sure they hadn't noticed him. He peeked around the wall. The two younger ones were leaving. They turned in the opposite direction. He waited for them to turn the corner before he stepped out of the safety of the office. He looked around to make sure nobody was watching. It was a busy station. All the people were too involved with their own shit to notice him.

He slowly worked his way back to where he had been standing before. He heard the older one talking. "You want me to check on this Jack guy? What was his last name?" He inched a little closer.

"Rivers. Jack Rivers. And I'll do it. You go help Ben and Jake get ready for Kate. I want to make sure everything is secure. I don't want this bastard anywhere near her."

He saw the door opening. He walked as fast as he could back to the other office. He didn't want to draw any attention. He had just turned into the office when he saw the older cop leave. His heart was racing. It had definitely been worth the risk. He now had a plan. He smiled. Very soon he would be with Kate, and then he would teach her a lesson.

The next day Kate was sitting on the couch in Jack's living room. She was nervous and antsy. She still couldn't believe the plan Jack and Paine had come up with, and they hadn't even checked with her about it first. She would have said no. It was crazy. She had to admit, though, it was a good plan. Crazy but good.

She had been upset with Jack at first, but when he had walked her through it, it had started to make sense. She just hoped everything went according to plan. She was still sitting there lost in thought when Jack came in from outside. He walked over to her, sat next to her, and took her hand. "Babe, I can see your wheels turning. Talk to me. What's wrong?"

She frowned. "What's wrong?" She took her hand out of his. "I know I agreed earlier about your plan." She looked at Jack. "I'm not so sure now. It could be putting you in harm's way." She stood. "And I can't still feel a little angry that you didn't talk to me about it first."

"Kate." Jack stood up too.

"Don't 'Kate' me. You should have talked to me first. I'm trying to stop people from getting hurt."

Jack reached for her hands again. "You're right. I should have talked with you first. You know it's a good plan, though. It makes the most sense." He put his arm around her shoulder and squeezed her tightly. "It's not me you need to worry about. It's not me he wants." She shuddered. "I'm sorry, Kate. I don't mean to scare you. What I'm trying to say is, you don't have to worry about me."

Kate could hear the fear in his voice. Kate turned and put both arms around his waist. "I know this is hard for you, but I have to do it." She leaned away so she could see his face. "If I don't do this now, we might never be able to be together. I'll always be running."

She reached up and brought his mouth down to hers. Passion, desperation, and fear filled the kiss. They kissed as if they would never kiss again.

Jack ran his mouth along her jaw, kissing and tasting her. "Kate, I can't lose you. Do you hear me? I can't lose you."

Kate entwined her hand with his and led him to the bedroom. "You're not going to lose me."

She prayed to God she was right.

# 17

Two days later Jack pulled into a parking space in front of the bar. Neither Jack nor Kate said anything. She kept her eyes on the bar, but she felt Jack turn to look at her. "You don't have to do this," he said. "You can get somebody else to cover your shift."

She turned to him and sighed. "It's okay, Jack. Everything will be fine. Besides, there is no one else to cover."

She scooted over to him. She took his face into her hands. "I owe Joe a lot. I can't flake out on him." She reached up and kissed him. "I'll have lots of people around me. I have your cell number in my phone. I'll be fine. I'll call if I need you."

Jack grabbed her and hugged her tightly. "I love you."

Kate felt the stinging in her eyes. She would not cry. Jack would never let her go if she started to cry. She laughed. "I love you too, Jack. But I can't breathe."

He released her immediately and grinned. "Sorry."

With one last look, Kate scooted over and hopped out of the truck. She was getting better at getting in and out of his truck. Kate looked around. She had that familiar feeling of being watched. She didn't see anything unusual. She wondered if she should say something to Jack. No. He would never leave her then. She knew he had things to do. It was probably just nerves. With one last look around, she stepped up on the curb and went into the bar.

There she was. At last. He watched as the truck pulled up in front of a bar. So this was Jack. He didn't look like anything special—just another guy thinking he was protecting Kate. He smiled. They had no idea.

They thought she was safe in this Podunk town, but once again he had outsmarted them. Lucky for him, this town was small enough that he could see most of it from where he was hiding. He knew where the boyfriend lived, but he didn't want to risk them noticing a car near his place. So he had waited, and here she was. He continued to watch. She was moving over to Jack. What was she doing? He watched as she kissed him. His fists clenched. The blinding rage made him want to go over there and pull her out of the truck by her hair. He took a step toward the truck. She was going to pay for that. He stopped. He told himself to be patient. Her time was coming. He was going to take his sweet time with her, too. He stepped back behind the wood post. He was smarter than that and smarter than they were.

He watched as she stepped out of the truck and looked around. He held his breath. She couldn't see him. He was sure. It seemed as if she were looking right at him, though. He stared back. After a moment she turned and went into the bar. He let out his breath. He was so close. He couldn't fuck it up now.

He waited for the boyfriend to leave. What was he doing? He was just sitting there. *Leave, fucker.* After a few tense moments he saw the truck reverse and leave. He didn't step out of his hiding spot until he saw the truck head toward the highway. He stepped away from his hiding spot and went for the bar. He wondered if she worked there. He was going to have to go in. He needed to figure out his options. First he would do a surveillance of the place.

He went around to the back of the bar. An alley ran behind the buildings. He looked up and down it. There were trash cans spread throughout. It was dirty and smelled like old garbage.

Not seeing anyone, he stepped into the alley. He found the back door of the bar and tried opening it. It was locked. He smiled. That wouldn't stop him. He had just stepped away from the door, when he heard a noise. Looking down the alley, he saw a man step out a couple of doors down. He stepped back and pressed himself as close as he could get to the bar door. Silently, he watched the man head for a garbage can sitting a few feet from where he was standing. He was carrying two large black bags. When he reached the garbage can, he put down one bag and lifted the lid. He swung the bag he was still holding into the can. He bent down and picked up the other one. That was when he knew the man had spotted him. The man stopped and slowly lifted his head. The man stared at him. He stepped away from the bar door and headed in the man's direction. When he was closer, he saw the man was in his late sixties with a big round belly. He was not a threat.

"What are you doing out here, boy?" the old man asked in a raspy voice.

Giving him his best "I don't want trouble" smile, he stopped in front of him. "I was in the bar and needed some fresh air."

The old man laughed. "Well, boy, you picked the wrong place for fresh air. Can't you smell it out here?"

He laughed back. "Yeah. It's pretty nasty."

The old man kept staring at him. "I don't think I've ever seen you around here before."

He stepped a little closer and looked around. "No, old man, I'm not from around here."

The man looked down and saw the knife, and then the man looked back up at him and frowned. The old man tried to step back, but he grabbed the old man's arm and plunged the knife into his fat stomach. He watched him as the man grabbed his gut and looked up at him with confusion.

"Sorry, old man. Wrong place. Wrong time."

He thrust the knife into his stomach again. The old man fell to his knees and tried grabbing his pant leg. In disgust, he backed away. He watched the man trying to crawl away. *Really? Why do they always think they can get away?* He looked around the alley again to ensure nobody else had decided to come out. Looking back at the man, he saw him fall for the last time onto his stomach.

He sighed and bent to pick up the old man's legs. He didn't need this right now. Dragging the man by his legs very slowly, he started back to the garbage can. The man had to weigh close to three hundred pounds. *Great. The fattest man in this God-awful town had to be the one to see me.* Breathing hard, he realized he wasn't going to be able to lift the old man into the can. He couldn't leave him out in the open, though. Somebody would surely see him. The game would be up before he'd even started. He looked around and once again grabbed the old man's legs.

When he was done, he stepped back. It was not the greatest plan, but it was going to have to do. He didn't have a lot of time here. He didn't know when Kate was leaving for Portland. He was brushing off his pant legs when he noticed the blood on his shirt cuffs. *Fuck. Fuck. Fuck!* Now he was going to have to change his shirt, and he didn't have time. He still hadn't been *in* the bar yet. He sure as hell couldn't go in there with blood on his shirt, though.

After one last look at the old man, he left the alley. When he reached the sidewalk, he stopped and checked the street. He didn't see anyone roaming the sidewalks and didn't see any cars coming down the street. He sprinted back to his car.

If his prize wasn't so close, he would have called it a day. The old man had screwed everything up. He knew he couldn't leave now, though. He wanted Kate. He smiled. *Soon, Kate. I'm coming.*

Kate was so tired, she couldn't think straight. It had been a busy night. She was so jumpy, she had dropped a drink on some poor guy's lap. Fortunately, he had been a good sport about it.

She talked to Joe and told him she had to leave. Kate swore she saw moisture in his eyes, and that made her want to cry. She knew her crying would have embarrassed him, though, so she hugged him and said she would try to come back as soon as she could.

He left shortly after that. He never stayed too long. Now it was just her and Amanda doing the nightly closing.

"Hey, girl. Some night, huh?" Not waiting for a reply, Amanda rambled on. "I'm beat. My feet feel as if I've been walking in high heels."

Kate looked down at Amanda's feet. She was wearing pumps with at least a two-inch heel. "I hate to break it to you, but you are walking in high heels."

Amanda looked down at her feet. "These? These aren't high heels. I could go jogging in these shoes."

Kate laughed and finished wiping down the last table. "Why don't you go home? I can finish here."

"Are you sure?"

Kate turned and looked at her. "I'm sure. There's not much left to do anyway. And Jack will be here soon."

Amanda was smiling. "Well, if you're sure. I kind of have a date tonight."

Kate frowned at her. "How do you *kind of* have a date tonight?"

Amanda was looking at her strangely. "You know? It was implied, but there's nothing official. I swear, girl. You need to get out more. Wait. If Jack Rivers were my boyfriend, I wouldn't ever want to go out either. If you get my drift." She wiggled her eyebrows.

Kate just shook her head. "Go."

She was surprised when Amanda pulled her in for a hug. "I'll miss you around here. It just won't be the same. I won't have anybody here who can kick some major butt."

Kate laughed and hugged her back. "I'll miss you too. And you know, you could learn how to kick some major butt."

Amanda stepped back. "I wouldn't want to break a nail or something." She winked. "Just kidding. Maybe you can teach me when you get back."

Kate truly hoped she was coming back. She had made some friends here, and the town felt like home to her. Of course, there was Jack, and maybe he was why it felt like home. They had never really talked about the future. She was sure she wanted Jack in hers, and she was pretty confident Jack wanted her in his. She had never thought about the future before. Now she knew she wanted one—with Jack.

She was still daydreaming about Jack when she heard Amanda say, "Okay, girl, I'm outta here. You be good, and I'll see you soon."

Just like that she was gone, and Kate was alone. She walked over and locked the door. She turned back and surveyed the room. All was quiet. She had never realized before how quiet the bar could be. Normally, she liked the quiet, but tonight it just made her even more nervous than before. She was always teasing Paine about having a heart attack. Now she felt as if she might.

Shaking off her nerves, she walked over to the bar. All she had left to do was wipe off the salt and pepper shakers and put them back on the tables. Then she could get out of here and back to Jack.

She was putting the last set of shakers on a table when she heard a noise. It sounded like a creak in the floorboard. Kate froze. Her heart started pounding. Her breath was coming in short bursts. Kate didn't move. She waited to see if she heard the noise again. She wondered if Joe had come back, but Joe would have let her know he was there. Kate waited but didn't hear anything. *Maybe it was nothing.*

Kate wasn't taking any chances. She pulled her gun from her waistband. She might be overreacting, but she didn't care. She felt better with the gun in her hand. She had to get to the bar and grab her bag, and then she could be out of there. Jack should be there by now. It would be easy if she could just get her legs moving. *One step at a time. You can do this.* She stepped toward the bar. One step. Two. She had just stepped around the bar when she saw it. A purple rose was lying on the bar. She didn't move. She couldn't think. Fear froze her. She felt as if her heart were going to explode inside her chest. She was sure the rose hadn't been there earlier. *How did he put it there? Wouldn't I have noticed?* She needed to get out. *Run, Kate.* If she could reach the door, she could run out, and Jack would be there waiting for her. She turned toward the door. Get to the lights. She heard steps behind her. She stumbled and almost fell, but she kept an eye on the door. The door was her safety. She was breathing hard as if she had just ran a marathon. *Keep going for the door, Kate.*

She was waiting for a hand to reach out and grab her. *Oh God.* She could feel him now. He was closer. Kate had just opened her mouth to scream when she heard him.

"Kate."

She remembered that voice. She had heard it in her head a thousand times. It was just a whisper, but it still sent chills down her spine.

"Kate, I want you to stop."

*Yeah, right.* Kate had heard that before. She turned her head. "Fuck you, asshole." She kept going.

"If you want to know what happened to Jack, you'll stop." He didn't whisper this time.

Kate stopped. *Oh my God. Jack. What did he do to Jack?* Fear numbed her. If anything had happened to Jack…she couldn't even let her mind go there.

Kate felt him behind her. She whipped around and pointed the gun. No one was there. She searched the room and aimed her gun wherever her eyes went. *Where is he? He was right behind me a second ago.* She started backing toward the door. Still not seeing him, she turned for the door.

"Remember Nick?"

She hesitated.

"Do you want the same fate for Jack?"

She looked at the door. She was so close to escaping this night-mare, but she couldn't leave until she found out what had happened to Jack. Taking a deep breath, she slowly turned around.

She didn't see him at first. Then she saw a movement in the corner of the room. She could feel his eyes on her. He was standing there calmly, looking at her. She still couldn't see his face clearly. Shadows partially covered him. "Why don't you come out where I can see you?" she said with false boldness. Holding the gun with both hands, she brought it up higher. She was steady and firm. "Where's Jack?" she demanded.

"Not so fast, my dear Kate." He sounded smug and condescending as if talking to a child. He started toward her. Kate watched as he stepped out of the shadows. For the first time Kate saw her stalker's face. The first thing that came to her mind was average. He was average height and average weight. His hair was a dull brown and parted on the side. It was not light brown or dark brown. It was just brown. His face was even average-looking. He wasn't handsome or unattractive. She probably wouldn't have even noticed him if she passed him on the street. She recognized his eyes, though. They were the same soulless eyes as before. They were looking at her now with hatred and betrayal.

"If you want to know about Jack, you'll drop the gun."

*Think, Kate. I could shoot him in the arm or leg.* He was still coming toward her.

"I know what you're thinking, and I wouldn't, Kate."

*Can I do it? Can I pull the trigger?* He was standing in front of her now. He reached up and took the gun out of her hands. Kate had lost her lifeline. *What choice did I have? He has Jack.*

He threw the gun behind her. Kate heard it sliding across the floor. She wanted to run after it, but she stayed where she was. She watched him. An ugly smile came over his face. "You were perfect, Kate. We would have been perfect together."

Suddenly he grabbed her arm and turned her around. She could feel his breath on her neck. It was the same foul nasty breath.

"Do you know how long I've been waiting for this?" She felt him sniffing her hair. "I have never forgotten your smell." Kate wanted to gag. He grabbed her hair and pulled her head back. "But you ruined it, Kate," he whispered harshly in her ear. He yanked her hair harder, and Kate cried out. She felt tears come to her eyes. "Now you're just like the rest of them. You whored yourself out."

She saw the knife flash. Kate felt the point resting on her cheek. She tried to pull away, but he still had ahold of her hair. She couldn't move her head. "Please tell me where Jack is," she pleaded.

He laughed. "We'll get to that, but first you're going to notice me."

He jerked her hair and pulled her back. Kate stumbled and fell. He was dragging her by her hair. She tried to get up. She tried to put her feet underneath her to stand, but her shoes kept slipping. Kate reached up to grab the hand he had wrapped around her hair. It felt as if he was pulling her hair out one strand at a time.

"You see, Kate," he continued, "I already know you. I know everything about you. Now it's your turn." He was breathing hard, but his hold was strong. "You have caused me a lot of trouble, Kate." He was panting now. "I have to say, I was surprised when you left."

He stopped and let go of her hair. Kate's head hit the floor. She saw stars. She didn't know which was worse—her hair being pulled out of her head or her head slamming on the wood floors. She was lying on her back with her eyes closed.

"Get up, Kate." He was back to whispering. When she opened her eyes again, he was standing over her. "I said get up." He kicked her viciously in the side.

Kate winced, still sore from the drunk incident a couple days ago. She was not going to let this asshole win, though. She would not let him know he had hurt her. She stood up very slowly. She felt nauseated. She felt as if a jackhammer were pounding in her head. She didn't know if it was from the hair pulling or from having hit her head. *Maybe I could puke all over him. That would show him. Death by puke.* Kate smiled.

"What's so funny?" he asked harshly. "Do you think this is funny?" He was getting angrier by the minute.

*Careful, Kate. Don't push him too much.* "I think you're funny." She laughed. "You sneak around in the dark as if you're some ghost." She stepped closer. "But instead all you are is a man whom nobody would notice."

He roared with rage. "You bitch. I'm going to kill you."

He came at her with the knife. As if in slow motion, she watched the knife come down. She put her right arm up to deflect it, and she felt the pain as the knife ripped down her arm. She cried out, but she was ready. She was moving in for her move. She had one shot.

Her heart was pounding, but she grabbed the arm holding the knife and twisted. The knife fell to the floor. She turned so her back was pressed up against his chest. She punched her elbow down into his stomach. She heard his cry of pain. She brought her foot down onto his. She turned again and put her knee into his groin. He doubled over in pain. Kate looked around for the knife. She was breathing hard. *Where is it?* She felt blood dripping down her arm. She tried to ignore the pain. She was still looking for the knife when she saw him stand up. Forgetting the knife, Kate started to run.

She had taken two steps when he tackled her from behind by the ankles. Kate fell hard to the ground. Her cheek smacked the floor. She was seeing stars again, but she immediately started kicking him. She got one leg loose. She hit him in the chest. He grunted but didn't let go. She kicked again. This time she hit his face. She felt her other ankle come loose.

She frantically started crawling away. She had barely moved when she spotted the knife under a barstool. She tried to stand, but her shoes kept slipping on the blood dripping from her arm. She tried standing again, but she landed on her elbow. She cried out in pain. She wanted to scream in frustration. Every part of her body hurt. With her heart in her throat, she started crawling. She was almost there. She reached for the knife. She had just reached the knife handle when he landed on top of her. She felt the air leave her lungs. She couldn't breathe. She was still trying to catch her breath when he started pulling her hair again. Her head was yanked back. Kate cried out in frustration.

"You stupid little bitch, do you think you're smarter than I am?" he yelled.

When Kate felt the air come back into her lungs, she tried to turn herself over. He was sitting on her back. She started thrashing around. Moving her body up and down, she tried to throw him off as if she was a bucking bull. He was holding on by her hair. Too exhausted, Kate went perfectly still. She didn't think she had any fight left in her.

"Now, let's try this again."

Kate felt his weight shift. Before she could move, though, he turned her over and was sitting on her stomach. Her arms were pinned down. The pressure on her hurt arm was excruciating. She was living the nightmare all over again. She started jerking her body around like a fish out of water. She didn't even realize she was screaming until she felt the slap across her face. She stopped moving.

"After everything I've done for you, this is how you act?" he said angrily.

Spittle was spewing from his mouth. She turned her head in disgust. She saw the knife lying a few feet from her, and hope flared in her chest. If she could get her left arm loose, she thought she could reach it. She turned back to him. She didn't want him to see the knife. She needed a distraction.

"After everything you did for me?" she fired back. "You haven't done anything for me."

His face turned into a distorted, ugly mask. "You ungrateful little bitch." His weight shifted. Her arm moved a little. She just needed a few more tugs. "The women, Kate. I killed those women for you."

"You didn't do it for me." Her arm moved. "You did it because you're a sick, demented asshole." Kate closed her eyes and waited for him to slap her again. Instead she heard him laughing.

"Oh, my sweet Kate." Kate couldn't keep up with this man's many changing moods. "I know that's what they told you, so I'm going to let that remark pass." He shifted. She moved her arm. "All I wanted was for you to notice me." He was back to the creepy whisper.

Kate decided to change tactics. "I would have noticed you. All you had to do was come talk to me."

"Why do keep treating me as if I'm stupid? You wouldn't have noticed me. That's why I wanted you to get to know me first. You were special."

Kate didn't understand. "If I'm so special, why are treating me like this?" She wanted to add *asshole* to the end of that question, but she didn't.

He chuckled. "Don't you get it yet, Kate? If you weren't special, you'd be dead already."

Kate felt cold all over. She knew she wasn't going to talk her way out of this. There was no reasoning with insanity. She was going to have to fight her way out. "Please. It doesn't have to be like this. Just tell me Jack is okay, and then you and I can go away together."

"Do you think I want you now? After you've been with *him*?" He snarled. "No. You're just like all the rest. You're not special anymore."

Kate felt his body shifting again. She knew she was running out of time. With one last pull, her arm was free. Not wasting a single moment, she reached for the knife. He saw her reach for it, and his evil eyes turned black with rage. He wrapped his hands around her neck and started squeezing.

Kate couldn't get a breath. She was fighting for air. He was squeezing the life out of her. Using her free arm, she grabbed his arm and tried to pull it away. It wouldn't budge. He was too strong. She gasped for air. Knowing her last chance was the knife, Kate reached for it. Stretching her arm as far as she could, she felt her fingertips touch the handle. *Just a little more.* She pulled the knife closer with her fingertips. She was starting to lose consciousness. She felt the blackness trying to take over. *It's now or never, Kate.* With one last effort, she wrapped her hand around the knife. She swung the knife toward his shoulder, but before she could bring her arm down, he lifted his arm and blocked it. She brought the knife under his arm and swung again. This time she made contact. She didn't care where she was aiming. She just swung. In her awkward position, the knife sliced down his face and then plunged into his neck.

He roared back in pain. The fingers wrapped around her neck came loose. She took in one mouthful of air after another. She still couldn't move, but at least she could breathe. She looked at her attacker. Blood ran down his face from an inch-long gash running down his cheek.

Kate gave him a cold smile. "Looks as if *you're* marked now, asshole."

In horror Kate watched as he reached for the knife and started slowly pulling it from his neck. He screamed in pain.

*No! No! No!* In a panic she started flailing her body around and trying to get loose. She didn't want to die. She wanted a future with Jack. She stopped moving when she heard him snicker. He was holding the knife in his hand. "You are as stupid as the others. I didn't do anything to your precious Jack." He wiped some blood off his face. "But now I think I'll kill them all." Kate watched as he lifted his arms into the air. He was holding the knife with both hands. "Do you notice me now?"

Kate screamed.

Jack watched as Kate went into the bar. He didn't know if he could leave her. How could he leave her with some maniac after her? He wanted to keep her close and protect her. She would probably laugh at that and tell him she could take care of herself. Then she would proceed to show him her gun. He had no doubt she knew how to use the gun. That didn't stop him from wanting to keep her safe, though.

Knowing he didn't have a choice, Jack put the truck in reverse. He had a meeting to get to. He pulled away from the bar and headed toward the highway. Jack was a little uneasy about this meeting, and he wasn't sure what to expect.

Not that it mattered. Kate was his, and he wanted her with him forever. He knew Kate loved him. They just hadn't talked about the forever part yet. They would catch this asshole threatening her, and then he would convince her she couldn't live without him. Simple.

Jack saw the turnoff coming up. Returning his focus to the upcoming meeting, he pulled into the campground. He had picked this spot because it was private and close to town. Also it would be easy to notice if anybody had followed him.

He pulled his truck alongside the only other car in the campground. He immediately saw the four men sitting at the picnic bench. They stood when they saw him pull in. Jack put the truck in park and jumped out. He walked toward them. They were all tall and about his age. Except one. He figured that must be Paine. To his surprise the one who stepped away from the others wasn't the older one.

"Jack?" the man asked. Jack nodded. The man held out his hand to shake. "I'm Paine."

They sized each other up. Jack shook his hand. "I expected you to be older."

Paine laughed. "I thought you would be better-looking." Jack grinned. The tension eased some. Paine turned and looked at the other men. "This is Ben."

The tall dark-haired man came forward and shook Jack's hand. "How's our girl?"

Jack tensed when a stab of jealousy hit him. He had to remember these guys were important to Kate, and Kate was important to them. "She's strong," Jack said, and Ben nodded.

Paine was pointing to the next guy. "This is Jake."

The blond man stepped closer. He reminded Jack of a surfer dude. "Good to meet you."

Jack tried to pull his hand back from the shake, but Jake didn't let go. "You break her heart, and I'll have to hurt you."

Jack started to smile but saw the man was serious. Jack cleared his throat. "Fair enough."

Jake nodded and let go of his hand. Paine pointed to the last man. "And this is Bill."

The man was older but still looked as if he could put somebody in the hospital. "You ready to catch this son of a bitch?"

Jack was surprised how softly he spoke. His eyes looked as if he were ready to kill somebody. Jack gave him the same look and released Bill's hand. "I'm ready."

With the introductions done, they all sat down at the picnic bench. Paine spoke first. "How is she?"

Jack was about to give a one-word answer, but as he looked around at the men who had protected Kate, he knew they deserved more. "She's hanging in there. She wants this to be over with, though. And she misses you guys." That put smiles on their faces.

"We sure miss her too," Ben said. "It's frustrating as hell we can't catch this guy."

Jack looked at Ben. "There's been nothing to figure out who this guy is?"

"There's no physical evidence, but our guts are telling us he's a cop." Paine ran his hand through his hair. "We know he's been hacking into my computer at work. Keeping an eye on us. Also, the way he's been killing those women. They were killed in places nobody should have been able to get to them. They must have felt they could trust him. Except the last one. She was found in an alley."

"What about the roses? Anything there?" Jack asked. He kept his voice neutral. He didn't want to upset these guys because they hadn't caught this guy. He knew from experience it wasn't as easy as it seemed on TV.

"We checked every flower shop in and outside the city limits," Jake said. "A couple remember selling purple roses to a man, but each description was different. So we think he changes his appearance. He never used the same flower store twice, and he always paid with cash."

"Paine, you said he's been hacking into your computer. You can't trace that back?" Jack knew it was slim, but he had to ask.

"I used a friend of mine outside the department who's a computer geek. A good one too. He said that whoever this guy was, he knew how to cover his tracks." Jack nodded. "That's why we hope this plan of yours works. My geek friend told me this guy hacked my computer again after our little acting performance."

"I think it will work," Jack said. "We just don't know how long he'll wait to make his move." Jack hoped it didn't take too long. He didn't know if his nerves could take much more. He feared for Kate. He wanted to rush back to her now. For this plan to work, though, he had to stay away.

"All I can tell you is that we left Kate unprotected for one day," Bill said. "And he was there." The venom he heard in the soft-spoken man's voice surprised Jack.

"Let's go over the plan one more time." Paine looked at Jack. "You said you were a cop?"

"Ten years."

Paine nodded. "Then I'm going to assume you know how to handle yourself." Paine was staring intensely at Jack, but Jack didn't look away. He gave him the same intense look back. No matter what this guy threw at him, he wasn't leaving Kate. After a long tense moment, it seemed as if Paine had come to some decision. "Because Kate trusts you, we're going to trust you. And it seems you care quite a bit for her."

"I love her, and when this is all over, I'm going to do my damnedest to get her to marry me." He couldn't think about his future if Kate wasn't in it.

Jake laughed. "Holy shit, Jack. Congratulations." Then the smile left his face. "But it doesn't change the fact that if you hurt her, I will still come after you."

Jack grinned. "Deal."

Jake looked at him and nodded. "Okay. Let's do this."

The men huddled around and started going over the plan. Jack went first. "I'll be waiting outside the bar for Kate. If I see the lights go out before twelve thirty, we go in. She's going to send Amanda home at midnight. That gives him thirty minutes to make his move." Jack tensed thinking about it. "Kate was sure he would want the lights out."

"The wuss." Jake snarled. "He can't get it up unless it's dark."

Paine agreed. "Every time he's made a play for Kate, it's been in the dark. I don't know if we should assume he'll do it that way this time, though."

Jack looked at him. "What are you thinking? He's getting bolder?"

Paine was shaking his head. "I don't know. He's been waiting a long time. I don't think he cares about the game anymore. He just wants her."

Jack stood. "I don't think this is such a good idea anymore." He started pacing. "What if he's coming for her now while we're sitting here twirling our thumbs?"

Paine stood too. "Jack, the plan is good. He won't come for her as long as she's with people." Paine stepped in front of him. "She's safe for now. If you can't keep your head in the game, then maybe you should stay out of it."

Jack glared at Paine. "I'm not going to sit on the sidelines. So don't even try that with me. If you try to stop me, I swear, I'll shoot you myself."

Paine glared back. "Then you need to calm down and start thinking like a cop again. Believe me, Jack, we all care for her. We have to catch this guy, or she'll never be safe," he said harshly. They stared at one another.

After a few intense seconds Bill stepped between them. "You boys done here? Because I would really like to catch this asshole."

Jack turned to Bill. All his anger left him. "You're right." He started pacing again. "She's safe for now."

Paine went back to the bench. "Okay. So Jack's out front waiting for Kate." He turned to Jake. "Jake, you and Ben will be in the back alley. If he comes in that way, we'll know."

Ben and Jake nodded in agreement. Jack was at the bench again. "You guys can't be seen. If he sees you, the game is up."

Jake stood and slapped Jack on the back. "Don't worry about us, Jack. He won't know we're there." Jack wasn't sure if he should be worried about the guy's cockiness. Paine seemed to trust him, though, so he figured he should probably trust him. "Bill and I will be across the street." He glanced at Jack. "We'll wait for your signal." He looked back to his men. "We don't go in unless we hear from Jack. Otherwise, we wait for another night."

Jack stopped pacing. "If he doesn't come tonight or tomorrow, Kate will want to go back to Portland."

"Jack, it might come to that. We don't know if he's here or if he's even coming."

"I know, Paine," Jack said more harshly than he'd intended. He wanted Kate here with him. Jack scrubbed a hand over his face. He had to quit taking his anger out on these guys. It was not their fault. "I'm sorry." He took a breath to calm himself. "I thought it would be easier if he came to us. A small town where people watch for strangers. Easier to see."

Paine stood. "We're going to get this guy, Jack. We're close. I can feel it." Paine started pacing. "He'll come for her, and when he does, we'll be there waiting."

No one said anything. They were all lost in their own thoughts. Jack was thinking about Kate and how scared she must be—alone at work and waiting for this guy to make a move.

Jack sat outside the bar and never took his eyes off the door. It had been the longest six hours he'd ever endured. Jack, Paine, and the others had waited at the campground until it was time to move. They had gone over the plan a couple of times, but after that everyone pretty much kept to themselves.

Jack had been sitting there since eleven forty-five. At midnight the bar door opened, and Amanda came out. She waved to him, got in her car, and left. Jack watched the lights in the bar. They were shining brightly. Jack looked at his watch. It was twelve fifteen. He had fifteen more minutes to wait, and then he could see Kate—see for himself she was safe and sound.

He heard Paine talking in his ear. "Jack? Anything?"

Jack checked his watch again. "Nothing. It seems quiet. The lights are shining nice and bright."

"Roger that," he heard Paine respond.

A couple of minutes later he heard Jake through his earpiece. "Um, guys, I think we have a problem." Jack sat up in his seat. Tension coiled through his body. "We have a body back here. It's an old man. It looks as if somebody tried to hide him."

"He's here!" Jack yelled into his mouthpiece. "Everybody, move. I'm going in."

His heart thumped in his chest, and Jack jumped out of his truck. He couldn't get to the bar door fast enough. He knew Kate was in trouble. The stalker had probably been in there with her while they were out there sitting on their asses. *The bastard's here. Please let her be all right.* He finally reached the door.

He tried the handle. It was locked. He was about to break down the door, when he heard Kate scream. A chill went down his spine. *He's in there. With Kate.* Not hesitating, he took out his gun and shot at the lock. He rammed his shoulder into the door, and it flew open.

What he saw made his blood run cold. Kate was on the floor, and the bastard was sitting on top of her. He was holding a knife above his head, and there was so much blood. A strong, blinding rage Jack never knew he possessed came over him. He ran at the guy and tackled him to the ground. He started pounding his fist into his face. He didn't stop. All he saw was this guy on top of Kate with the knife. He kept pounding. He was about to slam his fist into the guy again, but he felt arms going around his own.

"Jack, that's enough." He heard Paine's voice from far away.

All Jack wanted was to kill this guy. He tried twisting his arms to free himself. He got one arm free, and then he heard her. "Jack, please stop," she said softly. "He's not worth it."

*Kate!* He heard her. He had to get to her. "I'm done," he said. He was breathing hard.

He felt arms helping him up. Paine and Bill were watching him to make sure he wouldn't go after the guy again. He saw Jake and Ben putting handcuffs on the asshole. He wasn't moving. *Good.* Jack hoped he was dead. He turned to Kate. She was still lying on the floor, her blue eyes looking at him. He ran over and knelt down beside her. She reached up and touched his face. "I had this under control."

Jack laughed. He would never underestimate this woman's strength. "I know. It just felt good to beat the shit out of him." She smiled. "Babe, where are you hurt?" He felt his rage returning. Her cheek was starting to turn a bluish color. Her eye was puffy and swollen. Then he saw her arm. Blood covered it. "Kate, what happened to your arm?" He was afraid to touch her.

"It's not bad really. He just nicked me." Jack turned his head and kissed her palm. "It's over. It's finally over," she said, choking on her words.

He took her hand from his face and held it. "Yes. It's over. We need to get you to the hospital, though." He helped Kate sit up. "Not too fast." When he was sure she wasn't going to faint, Jack took off his shirt and started wrapping her arm. He couldn't see how bad the cut was through all the blood.

"Help me up, Jack." She was trying to stand on her own.

"Kate, I don't think that's a good idea."

"Please. I'm fine."

Jack knew she wouldn't give it up. He sighed, stood, and reached down to help her up with her good arm. He didn't let go. He had almost lost her. He wasn't taking any chances.

Kate still couldn't believe Jack was there. She had seen the door fly open and Jack plow into the guy, but it had all happened so fast. One minute she was being pinned down, and the next she was free. She watched as Jack kept grinding his fist into the guy's face. She knew he would have killed him if Paine and Bill hadn't stopped him. She hadn't known whether to believe the asshole when he had told her nothing had happened to Jack. *Here he is, though, helping me up. Nothing happened to him. Thank God.*

Kate felt a little woozy. She didn't think she was going to pass out, though. She looked up and smiled at Jack. "I love you."

"I love you too." He bent down and kissed her. They were still kissing when she heard coughing behind her. Reluctantly, they broke apart.

With a smile at Jack, she turned. She couldn't look at the man on the floor yet. Instead she looked at the four men who had become such important parts of her life. They looked the same. Paine looked a little older, but at least he still had some of his hair. Jake's hair was longer. She couldn't believe they were here standing in front of her. "Hi, guys," she said through tears. "I've missed you." They were all smiling.

She reached up to give Paine a hug and winced. Jack was immediately by her side. "Kate, what's wrong?"

She put her hand to her side. It came away with blood. She turned to look at Jack. "I think he stabbed me."

*When did he stab me?* With that last thought, blackness overtook her.

# 18

She could hear arguing. *Who's arguing? Where am I?* She felt the warmth of sunshine on her face. She opened her eyes to brightness. She had to blink a few times before her eyes would focus. She tried lifting her arm to shield her eyes, but something was holding her arm down.

"Kate, try not to move."

She turned to the voice and smiled. "Hi, Jake." Her voice felt scratchy. She cleared her throat. "How are you?" She sounded a little stronger that time.

"Darlin', don't worry about me." He touched her arm. "How are you?" He was wearing that cocky grin of his. Kate did not know how he was still single.

She continued looking around the room. Everything was white. The walls were white. Jake was standing to the right of Kate's bed, and the curtain behind him was white.

She turned her head to look at the other side of the room. She smiled. Ben was sitting in a chair in the corner of the room. His chin rested on his chest. He was sound asleep.

Jake followed her gaze. "Let's not wake him. He gets cranky."

"I heard that, jackass." Ben opened his eyes and smiled at Kate. "Hi, honey. It's sure good to see you." He left the chair and stood by her bedside. Kate reached for his hand, but with the IV attached to her arm, she couldn't reach him. He took her hand instead. "You look beautiful, as usual."

Kate snorted. "I'm sure. You must like the hospital gown look." She lifted her right arm. "And the mummy look." Her arm was wrapped from her wrist to below her shoulder.

"I'm just glad you're okay." He smiled down at her. She turned back to Jake when he took her other hand. "Yeah, darlin'. We're all glad you're okay. You did good. Real good."

"I don't know what I would have done without you guys for the last two years." She was wiping the tears away when Bill walked in.

He was shaking his head and frowning. "Those two are going to get arrested. Better yet, I'll arrest them myself," he said to no one in particular. He walked over to the bed and stood next to Ben. "They made you cry already?" He smiled.

Kate was shocked. Bill never made jokes, and that was two in less than a minute. At least she thought he was joking about arresting Jack and Paine.

"Hi, Bill. I was just telling these guys how much I've missed all of you."

Bill opened his mouth to say something, but the arguing in the hallway was getting louder. Kate scowled and turned to Bill. "What's going on with Jack and Paine?"

Bill was back to his serious self. "It's okay, Kate. I'm sure they'll be in as soon as they're done out there." Then she heard Ben mumble, "If they don't kill each other first."

Jake laughed. "It sure is fun to watch those two. They're like two dogs fighting over the same bone."

"What are they arguing about?" she asked.

She heard a female voice speaking in a stern but hushed tone.

"Uh-oh." Jake snickered. "Sounds as if they're getting in trouble."

Kate frowned at Jake.

"You know, darlin', I think you should dump this Jack guy. I'm much more pleasant."

Jack sneered as he came around the white curtain. Paine followed. "What the hell are you doing, Jake?"

Jake grinned. "See?"

Giving Jake an icy stare, Jack pushed his way in so he could stand beside Kate's bed. Still grinning, Jake moved to the end of the bed where Paine was standing. Jack picked up her hand. "Hi." There was no trace of irritation. "How you feeling?"

She smiled up at him. "I'm good." He bent down and kissed her gently. Kate felt it all the way to her toes.

Jack pulled away just enough to whisper, "I love you." Before she could respond, he stood and turned to the guys. She shifted to sit up straighter. She sucked in a breath. Her side was tight and sore. Jack turned back to her. "Take it easy, babe." He reached behind her and propped her pillows higher. "You have twelve stitches in your side. If you don't keep still, they're going to pop out."

She remembered now. Her side had been bleeding. "What happened, anyway? Why was it bleeding?"

"He must have stabbed you before I could get there." Jack's jaw clenched.

She reached up and touched his face. "You saved me, Jack." She looked at the other men in her life. "You all saved me." She looked at Paine. He was smiling at her. She smiled back. "You better come over here and give me a hug, or I'm going to get out this bed and come to you."

Paine made his way over to her. "Hey, kiddo. It's really good to see you." He bent over and kissed the top of her head. When he stood back up, he looked her over. "You look good."

She laughed. "You guys are good for my ego." Paine smiled, but the smile didn't quite reach his eyes. "What's wrong, Paine?" The silence was becoming awkward. Kate couldn't stand it anymore. She looked back and forth between Jack and Paine. "Do you guys want to tell me what you were arguing about?" She saw Jack stiffen. "I'm not some child who doesn't know how to take care of herself. If one of you doesn't tell me what's going on right now, I swear, I'm going to get my gun."

She heard Jake snort. She gave him an intimidating look. He laughed and put his hands in the air. "Hey, darlin', I'm on your side."

Paine was shifting on his feet. "Kate…"

Paine looked at Jack. Kate looked at Jack. Jack was glaring at Paine.

"Don't look at me for help. You know how I feel," Jack said. "But you might as well tell her and let her decide," he added in a more civil tone.

Paine looked around the room. He went over to the chair Ben had been sleeping in. He picked it up, brought it back to her bedside, and straddled it. She smiled when he ran his hand through his hair. She really had missed him.

She stiffened at his next words. "Kate, I'm going to ask you to do something difficult." He reached over and picked up her ice-cold hand. "But I'll understand if you don't want to." The more he spoke, the colder Kate got. She started shivering.

Jack noticed. He moved the covers up closer to her chest. She reached for his hand. He took it and squeezed. It gave her the strength she needed to hear what Paine had to say. "What do you need, Paine?" she asked in a voice calmer than she felt.

He took another deep breath. "Your stalker's name is Frank Dower. He's a computer analyst at a precinct in Tigard. He is a cop. He went through the academy, but he couldn't cut it on the streets. He'd had several disciplinary write-ups." She watched as Paine scrubbed his hand over his face. *At least it isn't his hair this time,* she thought.

"Apparently, if he made an arrest and a woman was involved, he would rough her up. But not all women." He looked to Jack and back to her. "The women he roughed up had long brown hair and blue eyes."

"Like me," Kate whispered.

Paine nodded. "So it started before you. He must have seen you somewhere, though, and his obsession took over."

Kate couldn't believe what she was hearing. This wasn't even about her. It was because she had the right hair and eye colors. "Do you think he stalked other women?" She felt Jack put his other hand on her shoulder.

"We do," Paine said. "He didn't stalk the last women he killed, though. He just wanted to get your attention."

Kate flinched.

"That's enough, Paine," Jack said angrily. Looking at Jack, Kate reached up and touched the hand resting on her shoulder.

"It's okay, Jack." She turned back to Paine. "In the bar he told me he had killed those women for me." Kate shuddered. "He said I was ungrateful."

"I'm sorry, Kate. I didn't mean to say it quite like that," he said uncomfortably. "What I meant is that we're sure he stalked other women before he stalked you." Jack was squeezing her hand again. "I don't want to upset you, but we don't think he let those women live."

Kate was trying to take it all in. *How many women? Why? What makes a man become a monster?* She turned back to Paine. "Do we know why?" She didn't know if knowing why would help, but she asked anyway.

"What he have found out so far is that his mother used to make him watch while she had male friends over." Paine said disgustingly. "According to the shrink his mother told him he would never be perfect so he better be good at something." Paine shook his head in disbelief. "And we can't find his mother and there is no record showing she died."

Ben answered. "Mommy issues," he said scornfully. "These people always seem to have mommy issues."

"Yep," Jake agreed. "But we caught his ass." He was smiling when he turned to Kate. "I mean, you caught his ass, darlin'."

Kate couldn't bring herself to return Jake's smile. It was still too fresh and too much to think about.

"That brings me to what I need your help with," she heard Paine say.

Kate braced herself. She looked at Jack warily. "It's okay, babe. I'm here with you." He squeezed her hand again. "Listen to what he has to say. If you don't want to do it, we go home."

Kate liked the sound of going home with Jack. Her nerves under control now, she turned back to Paine. "What do you need me to do?"

A week later Kate stood outside the government building in Cheyenne. It looked like every other government building she'd ever seen. It stood five stories tall, was painted a dull tan, and had a brick facade on its edges.

The weather had cooled off over the last week. The skies were gray and gloomy. Kate shivered as she stood there looking at the building. The tension in her stomach was making her queasy. It wasn't the outside of the building, though, that was making her nervous. It was what was inside. *Or who.*

She felt an arm go around her waist. She leaned into Jack's shoulder. He kissed the top of her head. "It's not too late to get in the truck and head back to Greenbluff."

"I would like to do just that more than anything." She smiled up at him. "With you." He gave her a heated look that quickly made her pulse rise. Just one look from him turned her legs to jelly. "But we both know I have to do this."

"Kate, you'll be safe." Paine brought her back to reality. "He'll be handcuffed and chained to the table. He can't hurt you. Jack and I will be outside the room watching."

"I know, Paine." *I'm safe.* She kept repeating that to herself. *I can do this.* She swallowed and straightened her shoulders. "Okay. Let's go."

Jack watched Kate through the one-way mirror. She had her hands in her lap. She was waiting patiently. It was for show, though. He knew she was scared, even if she would never admit it him. His heart twisted. He would have done anything for her not to have to go through this. He turned and glared at the man next to him. "I still think this is a bad idea. He's been killing for years. Leaving nothing behind to catch him. Do you really think he's going to be stupid enough to confess?"

"Normally, I would agree with you, Jack," Paine said. "But this guy is arrogant and conceited. Remember the notes? He wants us to know how smart he is." He ran a hand through his hair. "Kate was the one who got away. She made his world come crumbling down. I think he can't stand that," he said passionately. Paine looked back into the room. "And he asked to see Kate. In his warped mind, he thinks he can still have her."

Jack looked back at the room when he heard a door opening. He saw Kate tense, but she quickly relaxed her body. *Good girl.*

A guard came in holding Frank Dower's arm. Dower was dressed in an orange jumpsuit. His wrists and ankles were handcuffed. He had to shuffle his feet in order to walk. His face still had a few bruises that hadn't quite faded yet. Jack felt no remorse for beating him. *I'd do it again if he could. Bastard.*

The guard helped him to the table. Kate didn't say anything. She just watched him. Once he was seated and chained, the guard stood by the door.

Dower didn't talk. He just kept staring at Kate. He was trying to make her nervous. Kate, however, didn't give any signs of being anxious. She was staring back with an almost bored expression. Jack smiled. She was beautiful. He still couldn't believe she was his.

"I see you couldn't stay away," he said smugly.

Kate leaned in. "I came only to see your face." She gave the smallest hesitation. "I wanted to see what your face looked like knowing we had outsmarted you."

His face turned red with anger. Just as fast the anger was gone. "You have nothing on me, my dear Kate."

"You confessed to me that you had killed all those women," Kate said coolly.

"I did?" he said evenly. "It's funny. I don't remember that." It was his turn to lean in. "You didn't outsmart me. I'm still smarter than all of you."

Kate's brow wrinkled. "I must admit, I'm confused." She rested her hands on the table. "The police told me they found notes on women that said, 'Kate, do you notice me now?'"

He shrugged. "So? What's that got to do with me?"

"Well, only an arrogant, egotistical, conceited man would leave a note such as that." Kate laughed as she put her hands back in her lap. "You're right. You're too smart to leave a note like that. I mean, this guy is begging to be caught. Come to think of it, he's probably pretty stupid."

Jack saw the man clench his fist. *He's almost there, Kate.*

"And pathetic. Who wants an arrogant, egotistical, conceited man?" She lowered her voice as if about to share a secret. "And they told me he couldn't, you know, do it until after they were dead."

The man pulled at the handcuffs and tried to get to Kate. "Shut up. You're lying."

Kate didn't stop. She went on relentlessly. "I almost feel sorry for him. The only way he can get a woman is to kill her, and the only way he can get it up is after she's dead." She made a disgusted face.

He stood abruptly and knocked his chair over. "You bitch."

Jack started for the door, but Paine had ahold of his arm. "Wait, Jack. She knows what she's doing."

Jack looked back at the room. Kate seemed be holding up okay. In fact, she almost looked as if she was enjoying it.

"Do you think it's easy to not leave any evidence?"

Kate remained unflappable. "It can't be that hard. This guy did it, and we already determined he's stupid."

"You have no idea what you're talking about," he yelled. "I killed those women right under the cops' noses. I was standing right in front of them, and they didn't see me. Do you really think I would dirty myself by having sex with them?" His face was contorted in rage. "Nobody outsmarted me, and when I get out of here, I'll be coming for you." He was pushing the table inch by inch and trying to get to Kate. She stood up and away from him. The guard came over and pushed him back into his seat.

Jack was stunned. She had done it. He'd confessed. When he turned to Paine, Jack saw the same expression on his face. Paine looked over to him; a huge grin appeared.

Jack grinned back. "Now, can you please get her the hell out of there?"

# EPILOGUE

Three Months Later

**K**ate and Jack were sitting on the couch in Jack's living room, admiring the tree they had just cut down off his ranch. Jack had his arm around Kate's shoulders. "What do you think?"

She turned to look at him. Her eyes were glowing. "I think it's perfect. I'd never cut down a Christmas tree before."

Kate had been so excited when he'd told her that was what they'd be doing. She had been pretty picky about which tree to cut down. She'd wanted it to be perfect. They had been out most of the day finding the right tree. Jack hadn't complained. He'd patiently waited while she'd looked at each tree from different angles and decided if it was the one.

When they had returned to the ranch, Shane had helped Jack bring the tree in and set it up. Shane had left, but he and Avery were coming back later for dinner and to help decorate the tree.

Kate's life had changed so much in the last three months. After the confrontation with her stalker (she never used his name), she and Jack had returned to Greenbluff. Paine and the rest of the guys had escorted *him* back to Portland.

After he'd realized he had admitted to killing those women, the fight had seemed to leave him. He'd also confessed to killing the old man behind the bar. He had been the owner of the bakeshop down the street. Kate hadn't known him very well. His daughter had taken over the shop. She couldn't bring herself to go in there yet. One day, though, she would try to explain to his daughter why he had died.

The cops told *him* if he revealed Nick's location, they wouldn't seek the death penalty. Kate didn't believe in the death penalty, but after what he'd done to those women and Nick, she made an exception. He deserved to die. She had known in her heart Nick was dead, but she had always hoped he would magically appear. Eventually, he did tell them where to find Nick's body. Kate made the arrangements for Nick's funeral since there wasn't anybody else. It broke Kate's heart, but Jack, Paine, and the rest of the guys had been there with her. Her stalker would spend the rest of his life in prison.

Kate hadn't been back to the bar. She would face it soon enough, but she needed more time. She was back in school. She was taking online courses because there wasn't a university near Greenbluff. She was working part time at the diner as a waitress. She had started seeing a therapist in Billings two months before. The therapist was helping Kate deal with the guilt she felt about the women and Nick.

So once a week Jack drove her to Billings. She'd gotten her driver's license and thought she was a very good driver. However, when she told Jack she could drive herself to Billings, he turned that funny green color. So she let him drive.

She moved out of the apartment over the bar when Jack asked her to come live at the house with him. He told her she could stay in the spare bedroom if that made her more comfortable. Kate never used the spare bedroom once.

Kate helped out with the ranch when she could. Between school and her part-time job, it didn't leave a lot of time. She enjoyed the ranch, though. She also knew, if she was going to live there, she had a lot to learn.

She talked to Paine and the others every week. Paine admitted he had a date. "I have to tell you, Kate, I'm pretty nervous about it."

Kate smothered her laugh. "It's like riding a bike, Paine. Once you learn, you never forget." She couldn't wait to hear how it went. She was pleased he was getting over his ex-wife. He deserved to be happy.

Jake and Ben seemed to be in some contest to see who could date the most women. She had told them they should be dating, but she had no idea they would go this far. Every week she got to hear about the new girls they had just met, and then the following week she would hear about what was wrong with them. She knew when they found the right ones, though, they would both be loyal to a fault.

Bill was the same strong, quiet man, but even he took a spin at dating. He, of course, didn't say a lot about it, but it didn't stop Kate from asking.

Kate turned and kissed Jack on the cheek. "We'd better get dinner started. Avery and Shane will be here soon." She started to get up, but Jack held her back.

"Before we start dinner…" he croaked. Kate frowned. He seemed nervous. He started again. "Before we start dinner, I was wondering… or I was hoping…"

Kate had never seen Jack like this. He seemed unsure of himself. He was usually a strong, confident, take-charge kind of guy.

"I mean…" he continued. "I was going to wait until Christmas to give you this, but I can't wait any longer."

Kate looked down at what Jack was holding. She gasped. He was holding a square-cut diamond ring. She looked up at him, wide-eyed. Before she could answer, he jumped in. "I don't want to freak you out. I wanted to give you time. To adjust to being here with me. But I love you, and I want you to marry me." He let out a shaky breath. "I'll wait, though, if that's what you want. We can go as slowly as you'd like."

Kate put her fingers to his mouth to stop him from talking more. "Jack." She removed her fingers. "I love you too. Of course I'll marry you." He didn't say anything. He was just looking at her. "Did you hear me, Jack? I said yes."

The next thing she knew, she was in his arms. "God, Kate. I was so scared you would say no. After everything you've been through, I didn't know if it was too soon or if you wanted to get married at all." He was starting to ramble again.

She pushed him back and had to put her fingers on his mouth again. "I do have one condition," she said with a devilish grin.

Jack smiled. "What's that, babe?"

"You have to ask Paine for permission."

89204967R00113

Made in the USA
Middletown, DE
14 September 2018